GW00789893

THE INNOCENT AND COLLATERAL VICTIMS OF A BLOODY WAR WITH RUSSIA

short stories

by
Liviu Antonesei

Translated from the Romanian by
Mihai Rîșnoveanu, Mike Phillips and Ramona Mitrică

PROFUSION GOLD

Profusion, London 2014

PROFUSION GOLD SERIES

Liviu Antonesei - *The Innocent and Collateral Victims of a Bloody War with Russia* (short stories)

Stelian Țurlea - *Greuceanu – Novel with a Policeman* (novel)

Augustin Buzura - *Report on the State of Loneliness* (novel)

Series Editor: Mike Phillips
Published by Profusion International Creative Consultancy
mail@profusion.org.uk • www.profusion.org.uk

The Innocent and Collateral Victims of a Bloody War with Russia
by Liviu Antonesei
Published originally in Romanian as *Victimele inocente și colaterale ale unui sîngeros război cu Rusia*
Polirom, 2012

Cover photo by Laura Lazăr; Photo author: Eugen Harasim
Typesetting by SGS Creative
ISBN-13: 978-0956867650

Liviu Antonesei

THE INNOCENT AND COLLATERAL VICTIMS OF A BLOODY WAR WITH RUSSIA

CONTENTS

Introduction

Liviu Antonesei is best known as a radical poet and critic. On the other hand, his fiction reveals a well developed, sophisticated, almost knowing prose style. To begin with, the titles of his stories set up an atmosphere of intrigue. Take, for instance, *"The Innocent and Collateral Victims of a Bloody War with Russia, which, in the End, Did Not Take Place"*, and, *"Report on Two Couples Uprooted from Reality, Accompanied by a Vague, Imprecise Commentary Regarding Reality as Such."* On the surface these titles are a summary of the stories' events, but they actually pose questions which, slyly carve out a pathway through the playful narratives, and take the reader to the heart of Liviu's intention.

The stories themselves are a montage of factual observation and inquisitiveness, married to an acute insightfulness and a daring post-modernist style. They offer a radical perception of change and movement throughout Europe from a pair of fresh eyes, enlivened and enthused by the watershed of European accession. Liviu, however, is setting out to achieve something even more personal and deeply felt. Each story explores some aspect of memory in which family life, the life of the community, and the events which define life in the nation are mingled.

"I admit it," Liviu says of his fiction, "I usually lie to my readers and, as much as possible, I try to lie to them beautifully. I invent characters starting from a strange nose, or from the movement of a woman's bottom, then I embroider the stories around these elements according to the way my imagination runs. And I always try to give them an air of implacability - things cannot be otherwise - of authenticity. This time around, I want to be as honest as possible to my readers, my goal being to extract the characters straight from reality and try to reconstitute their stories from real facts, and to limit my imagination as much as possible."

Mike Phillips

The Innocent and Collateral Victims of a Bloody War with Russia which, in the End, Did Not Take Place

Some months had passed since my mother's departure from this best of all possible worlds, so I had finally decided, and found the time, to put in some order the papers left behind by her and my father – his departure having taken place almost three years earlier. I had already arranged the inheritance with my sister, while the clothing and other objects of personal use had been disposed of on the occasion of the several series of *parastas* commemoration masses and *pomană* alms-giving which animate the life of the dead for us, the Orthodox Christians, no matter what the extent of our religious devotion may be. I was wearing my mother's small and elegant golden cross, hanging from a narrow little chain. This was the cross which had accompanied her last years of life, while my sister had one of mother's rings on a finger of her right hand.

We had made a first sorting of the books a little while after the funeral, before putting the flat up for rent for the first time. We shared them out more or less equally, with some being taken by me or my sister, some being left on the spot, and some being given to others, or simply left on some plastic sheets near the area where we left the rubbish out, so that anyone could take a selection of books according to their interests and needs. We had also looked through the albums of photographs, and through the boxes in which other photos were stored, also sharing these out without many difficulties, because there were two or three copies of many of the images.

I was now alone in the small flat, surrounded by cardboard boxes of various origins and dimensions, and by plastic bags filled with papers. They were not dusty because they had been sheltered in the enclosed spaces of bookshelves, in wardrobes, and in all kinds of drawers from the sideboard and other pieces of furniture. There was a lot of furniture – but not too much – in this last flat of my mother's, because she was able to judiciously utilise the space in the room, in the bathroom, in the kitchen, and the hallway which was almost as wide as the room itself, and had been transformed into a kind of living room. So the flat did not have the usual clutter found in houses belonging to the old, because she had only kept a small part of the furniture from the spacious, three-room flat in which she'd lived with my father immediately after the big earthquake of 1977. This was the flat which she'd left, around a year after his death, in order to return here, approximately across the road from the house which had been demolished on the occasion of the earthquake, where I spent a great part of my childhood, my teenage years, and the beginning of my first youth among equal numbers of Romanian and Jewish families. A large family of Gypsies also lived among us – they were good, honest people – and Costache was part of this family. He was a boy around my age who would later become - after the earthquake and after we'd spread to the four corners of the town, drifting apart from each other a little - slightly less good and honest. Then he died a little time after being released from one of his many visits to the entrails of the prison system. He'd had many periods of incarceration there, all of them short-lived, because his offences were not grave: pilfering in the many workplaces, where he didn't stay long because there was something of a vagrant in him, even if he'd finished the mandatory period of school at some kind of vocational institution. As people said back then, and as they have started to say nowadays too, he was not integrated, despite the fact that he was a settled third-generation Gypsy.

So, I was sitting comfortably on the bed in my mother's room, surrounded by the boxes and packs of papers she had somehow archived, but not always according to the clearest and most rigorous criteria. I had arranged them in two categories: those I wanted to keep, and those that were to be given up to oblivion. It was not easy to do this because I was not proceeding in a clear enough manner either. Instead I was classifying things according to the impulse of the moment. As a result I decided to make a rather loose selection, which would be possibly followed by another, more thorough one once I got home, rather than risk leaving behind papers whose loss I would later on regret.

I would be unfair were I not to admit there had been a certain spirit of orderliness, even if it hadn't been perfect, in my mother's manner of doing things. Just as I had found the previous summer, the roughly grouped collections of photographs, the letters and postcards were also gathered together in several piles. Amongst these, in a box of bonbons tied with string, there were several tens of letters which I had sent during the six months of my army service, and, around halfway, they contained the earthquake I have already mentioned. I did not open any of the envelopes, not because

I lacked the curiosity – which was great, but because I did not want to interrupt the primary process of selection. I still haven't looked through them, not because the curiosity disappeared in the meantime, but simply because I want to avoid the reawakening of certain emotions for a while longer.

I kept other letters because of the people who sent them, just as I did with the thousands of illustrated postcards and greeting cards received with the occasions of name-days, birthdays, Christmas, Easter, 1st or 8th of March[1]. I am not a collector of postcards, but a collector of memories! As a consequence, only those from close members of the family were left. I was touched by the writing in some letters received from my grandparents, Toader and Zenovia, my mother's parents. It was neat handwriting, even beautiful, although neither of them had graduated from more than primary school, around the beginning of the other century, at the end of the other millennium. There were also some cards from old friends of my parents', whom I happened to meet while they were still on this earth. It is interesting that, in general, my parents outlived these people, as well as the majority of their own brothers and sisters. Even when I go to the cemetery, less often than is the custom, I always feel a kind of selfish satisfaction on seeing my parents surrounded by younger dead people, some of them much younger than they were. Is there something consolatory in this? I do not know, but this is how I encourage myself, although it is probably not the most Christian thing to make this kind of

---

1   In many Catholic and Orthodox countries, Romania included, people celebrate the feast day of their patron saint, hence the name-day. 1st and 8th of March are the most important non-religious celebrations in Romania, marking the arrival of spring and mothers' and women's day respectively.

comparison.

They had a passion for composing crosswords, which had occupied their time, especially after they retired, and the papers that had resulted from this hobby were grouped together in squared exercise notebooks – it was easier to draw the frames in them – but also in several folders. In addition, I also found the accounting papers of their crosswords magazine from the beginning of the transition[2], when they had caught, not quite the spirit of investing or the capitalist initiative, but rather the desire of editorial independence – if I may put it that way. As it happened, having been conned by the press distributors, they didn't grow rich but accrued debts with the printing houses, debts which they slowly paid off out of their pensions, since they had taken responsibility for the investment with dignity and accepted no help in the matter. In a plastic bag, there was an ink-pad and the rubber stamp of the "business" they had conducted in full legality! I decided to keep them. In other bags there were all sorts of membership cards and IDs: from the Red Cross, for being a war veteran and the wife of a war veteran, the card for pensioners with free passes on urban public transport, membership cards for various organisations – among them the cards of PAC[3] members, with the membership fees paid up to date! Then there were my mother's tens of little memo pads, agendas and agenda-notebooks of all dimensions and all kinds. Inside these notebooks, were mingled telephone numbers, addresses, financial calculations, poems, attempts

2 In contemporary Romanian parlance, "the beginning of transition" means the early 1990s, when the democratisation process started as a consequence of the 1989 revolution.

3 PAC – *Partidul Alianţa Civică*, the Civic Alliance Party, a 1990s attempt at an intellectual-driven, civic minded political force. A great part of Romania's intelligentsia of the time was in the leadership as well as the rank and file.

at childhood and youth recollections, notes about medical treatments or about writers Mircea Eliade and Marin Preda, a sentence or just a single word fixed on a page that otherwise remained blank, looking mysterious and enigmatic in their loneliness. A little note on which I recognised my handwriting in pencil fell from a notebook: "glasnost, sincerity, transparency; perestroika, restructuring". This was written around the end of the 80s, at the time when, after my divorce, I had lived with my parents. I don't know any more if I'd made that note for me or for one of them. Notebooks, agendas and memo pads. I kept them all and at some point I will have to rifle through them with care, just as I will have to explore the genealogical tree showing some four or five generations, composed by my father before he died.

It is interesting how we start to look for our origins when we feel our end is getting nearer. And just as interesting are the things that stay behind us after our goods, the objects that accompanied us during our lifetime, are inherited or given away. I always notice the papers, and especially papers, all kinds of papers, but what did survive back in the day when paper was not so common, so excessively used, so wasted ultimately? It was the memories, of course, what else could have stayed behind? On the other hand, was memory really stronger then than it is now, when it is exactly these papers which constitute some sort of crutch for our memory, trying to support its instability, its imprecise character, its holes?

I think that two envelopes and a postcard fell from the last notebook I rifled through hurriedly. The envelopes had dedications on them: "To Father, on his birthday", "To Mother, on her birthday (with apologies for the delay)", and inside them there was a poem for each! I don't think

I made any other such dedications to them! I don't think I even intentionally showed them one of my poems! They were dated 26 October 1989, so it was father's name-day and some weeks after my mother's name-day. The precise hour was also written down, even mentioning the minute when I'd finished the poems. They were handwritten, not typed. Were I not suffering from a certain bashfulness, I'd quote them here, but I don't believe any longer that they are poems. I think they are, instead, some existential documents connected to the special biographical-political situation in which I found myself during the autumn of that year. They were, in fact, somewhat lyrical signs of gratitude for the care they showed me in those circumstances, and for everything they had done for me since I had arrived skinless in this world. Oh yes, I had been quite skinless, not fully formed, since I had arrived without skin but armed with a front tooth. I was going to become incarnate only later on! I have the sensation that they were closest to me during that time when I stayed locked indoors and almost did not leave my room, just as I now feel their absence in the strongest and most acute way. Then there was the illustrated postcard, in fact not quite an illustrated card but a simple, cheap postcard worth 30 *bani*[4], produced on thin, low-quality paper with an already printed stamp that reproduced the crest of the RSR[5]. It was sent by me on 19 August 1968, written in synthetic pencil – I had probably found nothing else in the house of my relatives in the village where I'd gone on holiday a couple of days previously, after having been to the seaside with my mother and my sister. I have no idea why the two envelopes

4   Bani – subdivision of the Romanian currency Leu; 100 bani = 1 Leu.

5   RSR – Republica Socialistă România, the Socialist Republic of Romania

and this postcard were put together in the notebook, I only know that, without my realising it, I felt that I was slipping inside a kind of time tunnel. So it was 19 August 1968 when I wrote the postcard in which I told them I'd arrived all right, although they had just brought me there themselves a little earlier; that I was feeling wonderful, that I had become a true champion at eating watermelons. That postcard had been sent by me two days before I found that politics and history existed, and the postcard had probably reached them that very day, given that it had been sent within the limits of the same county! I do not think the three documents were together because of this. I have no idea whether mother was aware of the date when historical conscience awoke in me – if this formula doesn't sound a little too precious; but it is nevertheless interesting that the documents were together. At a distance of twenty-one years, they marked a beginning and a sort of crowning moment. Somehow this moment would have been about the debut of a historical conscience and, then, about my decision to move through history by means of self-liberation, by changing, unsettling, and by almost breaking my ties to the context, if I exclude the context of the family and make an exception for a very small group of friends and for a lover. It's more or less terrible to see how few people are left around you – as if you were afflicted by the plague or carried cholera – at the time when you really need to feel the presence of as many people as possible, even if that presence is diffuse and discreet. But while we are born alone, if we don't happen to be twins, and we leave this place even more alone, why should we feel legions of dear ones gathered around us in between the boundaries of this unfairly short interval? In fact, our solitude is probably normal, it is actually better that things are like this and not otherwise, and why should I complain. Haven't I always said I was irritated by camaraderie, by committee-ism, by the spirit of gregariousness? Haven't I condemned them, ever since I was very young, as signs of inferiority, as displays of plebeian attitudes, and maybe as indications of the inability to confront the loneliness of this world?

On 21 August 1968, I, and my two cousins on my mother's side, had woken up early, almost at the same time as the sun that tickled my eyelids, up there on the lookout of the thatch cabin, which was tied to a triangular wooden frame, and on which I had spent my hours of sleep. I was up in the lookout, they were in the cabin, my uncle was in the other, boss's cabin, the dogs were in their wooden kennels on the sides of the watermelon plantation, and the cows were under the skies, in the *no man's land* between the plantation and the nearby field of maize. We had fallen asleep early and we had partaken of a leaden sleep – at least, that is to say, we, the youngsters. Nobody had attacked the watermelons overnight, and the dogs had been quiet enough. I had fallen asleep with my eyes fixed on the skies, trying to recognise the constellations on the pitch-black surface. We had slept well, deeply, but one reason for waking up so early was because my uncle had granted us, one day previously, and somehow as a prize, a half-day leave during which we'd been out bathing in a pond located precisely on the other side of the village, on the shores of the Miletin rivulet; a beautiful name, with a vague Greek resonance. It was a well-deserved prize, of course, because on the previous day we had made a name for ourselves by picking the watermelons that were loaded into <u>two lorries and</u> several horse-carts, then sent by the CAP [6]

6   CAP - *Cooperativa Agricolă de Producție,* Agricultural Production Cooperative; general name for the cooperative farms organised by the communist state using the model of the Soviet kolkhoz

to the market in town. So, we had woken up early, we were relaxed, and we ate some homemade bread (that had started to go stale) with cheese, the remains of a roast chicken and some tomatoes, and then we began the first tasting session of the day. My uncle had left for the village in order to get cigarettes, so, by the time we reached a watermelon which seemed to be to our taste, with very green, shiny skin and small, black, especially widely-distributed pips, we'd already ruined some four or five, which had been sunk down the well during the previous evening in order cool them. We had thrown the remains of these other watermelons to the cows, in order not to be caught in the act of being prodigal. We were all seated on some sheepskins around the fireplace in front of our cabin, each one of us lazily tasted the red, cooling, and very sweet flesh of the fruit, holding a slice of watermelon in the left hand and a small knife in the right. Although it was still morning, the weather was turning increasingly hotter and we were discussing how we could convince my uncle and their father to grant us another half-day's leave for bathing. Up to that time, there were not many times in my life when I had lived through a beginning of the day which was so quiet, peaceful and kind – and I wasn't going to live through too many like it afterwards. It was as if the air itself stood still, almost compact and viscous. You need a day like this in order to understand, in the most physical and most meteorological manner, the poet's formulation of "still glory". I can assure you, being so dependent on the variations of weather, on climatic changes, that the meteorological sense is not one that deserves to be scorned or ignored. Well, in this full quietness, in this still glory, history invaded us; it invaded me – unexpectedly, like a lightning bolt! It invaded us under the guise of my cousin, the sister of the two brothers, whom we all saw running, going off the track in the maize field, her long hair flapping behind her, getting closer to us with a speed of which we would not have suspected her to be capable. We realised something had happened, but we had no idea what exactly it could have been in order to turn her into such a good runner of cross-country trials. She covered the distance under our eyes, wide with wonder, in a matter of some tens of seconds; she stopped in front of us, standing up spontaneously and somehow automatically, and said in one breath: "The Soviet army and those of another four brotherly countries have occupied Czechoslovakia!". I can still see her, even now, talking in between gasps for air, answering our not very skilled questions! I remember I was also following with interest her breasts, which were jumping up and down under her shirt, a fact from which you can see that the interdiction of incest is a late acquisition not just of the species, but also, in part, of each individual. Anyway, she looked very "sexy" to me – a word I had learned fast enough after we'd moved to town.

In the end, we understood that the other countries participating in the invasion were Hungary, Poland, Bulgaria and Germany. We did not really understand what our army had been doing, as it was not together with the others, and it was not clear either about which Germany we were talking, as two of them existed back then. In the end, I, being a little bit of a city dweller, was inclined to believe it was the GDR[7], a fact which was rigorously exact and respected historical truth. But the real problem was that

---

7   GDR – the German Democratic Republic, better known as East Germany, the communist side of the country.

I had to go immediately to the village in order to pick up my luggage, which had been already packed by my aunt, so that my uncle could drive me in a cart or the CAP's gig to the rail station in the neighbouring village, then get me on board a train and send me home, where my father would wait for me in Iaşi train station. This was so that I could be with my family *"if the Russians barge in on us, too"*. This formula sounded pretty strange in the mouth of my female cousin, who, despite the agitation that enveloped her, was only a girl, one or two years older than us. In fact, she was just a kind of Hermes of the female gender. She had just brought us the news running fast and in a hurry, as they used to say in those ancient places; and she had not made up the message herself.

In one hour's time I was in the gig, in another hour's time in the train station, and soon afterwards on the train bound for Iaşi. My father was not in the station, so I took energetically to the road home, which was situated less than a quarter of an hour's distance away, in the centre of the city. Once home, I found the living room full, and all present had their eyes fixed on the TV set: my father, grandmother, my sister, several neighbours who did not own a telly, and one of my mother's brothers. Not my mother, she was in Bucharest with a petition against some institution with which we shared the building, and which planned to take over our cellar and convert it into a storage area. Naturally, none of us would have agreed with the conversion, and least of all me, who had found in its hundreds of square metres and three descending levels a wonderful location for exploration. It was even a good place, better than the roof of the nearby block of flats, for secret encounters with Lili the Gypsy, Tamango as the folks in our apartment building called her. On the

TV they were broadcasting patriotic music, and they had a communiqué playing on a loop, which condemned in strong terms, as far as I could tell, the occupation of Czechoslovakia by the armies of the five "brotherly" countries. They also announced sporadically that there would be a rally in *Piaţa Palatului*[8] during which our Daddy[9] was going to formulate clearly Romania's point of view with regard to the event that had taken place overnight. The discourse eventually took place, and I have to admit I was impressed. Although the speaker was a bit of a stutterer and mangled his words now and then, he was convincing, energetic, mobilising, and somehow magnetic. You could also see this from the images in the square which was occupied by hundreds of thousands of people, from the applauses, cheering, and the slogans they shouted; but you could also see it in our little living room! How could it not have been so, as I saw my father more excited than ever, as a neighbour had his eyes open as wide as if they'd popped out of his head, and as I heard my uncle shouting he would go and join the patriotic guards, whose formation had been just announced by the speaker? Even my grandmother – who I don't believe recalled the name of any national leader since her Franz Josef – even she seemed enchanted by the magic of that discourse, and by the over-excited atmosphere of the images on the TV. Oh, yes: our Daddy was living his days of glory, given that he produced such an explosive impact from *Piaţa Palatului*

---

8 *Piaţa Palatului* – Palace Square, in front of the former royal palace in Bucharest. A place well-loved by Ceausescu for his political rallies in later years (his last one taking place on 21 December 1989, when he had to withdraw because of people's booing).

9 Our Daddy – a formula meaning Nicolae Ceauşescu, General Secretary of the Romanian Communist Party (from 1965) and President of Romania (from 1977), de facto ruler (dictator) or the country. He was often referred to, in propaganda, as "Father of the Nation".

right into our living room! Furthermore, after the discourse we all seemed shattered but convinced, and tightly united around our Leader – a formula which was going to have a long career in consequent public language. After the moments of stupefaction and compact silence, the grown-ups started to discuss; my sister and grandmother went to their rooms, and I lingered a little with the men who tolerated me, treating me as one of themselves. I expressed my opinion a couple of times, also being – what a surprise! – taken into consideration, but I was restless. The words about the popular guards, about the war of the entire people and the decisive riposte we would give to any aggression; these words did not give me peace. It seemed pretty clear that our turn would come after Czechoslovakia, although I had no idea why was this supposed to happen: maybe because we'd missed taking part in the overnight attack? Nevertheless what did I know? I had just turned 15 some months previously! In addition, I had been sitting quite peacefully that morning in the watermelon plantation located at less than fifty kilometres distance from Iaşi! On the other hand, if this was about us being attacked, if we were talking about the war of this entire people, then we ought to be prepared. All of us should be prepared for it. I quietly sneaked out of the room, then out of the house, in order to gather in some manner the small army of our courtyard, and of the few courts united around a small street running in parallel to the boulevard. The majority of the boys already knew what it was about. As it was already pretty late, we decided to meet again the next morning at 8, each of us bringing whatever we found at hand with regard to ammunition and weapons; after which we separated, going to our respective houses...

I slept quite badly and agitatedly, throwing away then

searching for the sheets with which I was covered, always changing the position of the pillow, and the disquiet, agitation and exaltation, all acting together, did not desert me, almost at all, during the course of the night. You could also hear the noise of heavy traffic coming from our main street: lorries, maybe even tanks, a thing that did not normally happen, because our street, as well as the whole city, usually seemed to be fully asleep before midnight. I was woken up by the voices of my father and mother – so she had reached home. It was earlier than I had planned, because I could hear the voices coming quite animatedly from behind the opaque glass doors separating my room in that old Jewish house (which was going to be demolished some ten years later along with other Jewish houses under the pretext of the damage caused by the earthquake). It was a space where I had felt very well for some fifteen years of my life, from the end of my primary school until I graduated from university. Let me return, however, to the morning of 22 August 1968 and the voices of my mother and father. At first, I eavesdropped from behind the glass doors on my mother's story about the rally. Although an entire night and a long journey by train had passed in the meantime, she seemed as excited as we had been, the folks in the Square and those in our living room, as excited as she had probably been down there in the Square – where, by chance, she happened to be for all the duration of the wait and then the delivery of the speech! Well, so I now heard that the people there (she talked about more than 300,000 people, if not even half a million, but I don't know according to what sources), had been in a state of delirium for the entire duration of the speech, and they didn't really want to go home when it ended; they had to be encouraged to go by the militiamen. I

also heard that she was going to join the Communist Party
– she, the daughter of well-off peasants who because of
her background could only attend midwifery school, and
even that only under the fictitious pretext of having been
adopted by a poorer relative! As I was going to learn later
on, this had also happened to grander houses, the case of
Goma[10] and other former political prisoners being the most
striking. Why did she want to join the Party? Well, in order
to be part of the patriotic guards and to fight the Russians!
God forgive us, it was the same reason as in the famous
cases mentioned above! It was clear my father was much
more sceptical and he even dropped sarcasms. When my
mother realised this she got angry and said: "What do you
know? You weren't there", which, in fact, was rigorously true,
but it did not necessarily contradict my father's scepticism.
However, I recalled at the time that he had grown incensed
enough during the televised broadcast of the speech, but
night had been a good counsel and brought him back to
his usual scepticism on all worldly matters – if not to his
proverbial lack of interest, which had barely been scratched
by my mother's stories. However, her words reminded me
that I had an army to organise, so I looked quickly at the
watch (it was 7.30), rapidly put on my shorts, my Chinese-
made tennis shoes with soles that lasted longer than those
of the Romanian-made ones, and a blouson. I ran out
past them, but I was stopped by my mother to give her
a welcome kiss. I kissed her, entered the kitchen, spread
butter and fruit preserve on some slices of bread, poured
cold milk in a cup, and threw everything down my throat.
When I looked at the clock on the kitchen wall I saw it was

10 Paul Goma – Romanian writer, born in 1935; a vocal opponent of the
communist regime and Ceaușescu.

almost ten to eight. From behind the curtains I saw that the boys had started to gather in front of the metal doors at the entrance to our cellar. I stalled a little, because a commander of armies arrives when the hosts are already gathered, but I still had to get there before Adolică did, because he would not have lost the opportunity to contest my title as he had on previous occasions. Certainly, now, just as in other times, I had the great advantage of this perfect fort that was the cellar, and I could also tell the others what I had heard from my grandmother. As I was going to confirm during the course of my life, my intuition was good. Those who have the story, also have the power, and I really had the story back then. I even had the initiative to get us organised with a view to resistance in front of the invaders, we were talking here about the war of the entire people, weren't we? What the devil!

When the kitchen clock showed 8 sharp, I exited the house quickly, went around it, reached the front of the cellar entrance and, realised from one quick glance of experienced leadership that almost all of us were there, almost all the combatants. We had left out those who were not yet in third grade in school[11], and we had left out those who were older, so that they could look after their girlfriends. In any case, if Willy, Costel or Gabi had agreed to take part in the war, any one of them would have asked for the position of commander of the hosts, and that was not possible! As a consequence, we were almost all the kids from around ten to fifteen years of age, some twelve fighters, without Adolică – a short version of Adolf, what a name his Jewish parents had chosen for him - who had not come and was

11   Third year of school in the Romanian school system; it means children aged around 8 or 9.

not going to come again. No, he was not at all cowardly, we'd always had fights between us, but I had gathered too many trump cards and the role of subordinate didn't agree with him. I unlocked the padlock, opened the massive, rusty metal doors, went in and turned the lights on. I waited for all of them to get inside, then I closed the doors – you're not organising such an important military operation in full view! The Russians, and we knew this from Uncle Vladimir, himself with some sort of Russian origins, had satellites that watched everything happening on Earth, down to the dimensions of a field tennis ball. The Americans could have watched any object down to the size of a Ping-Pong ball, but our problem was not with the Americans, despite the things normally written in the papers about American imperialism and its evils. What's more, they were very busy in Vietnam. Well, when all of us were inside, hidden from the indiscreet eyes of the enemy, we started to draw up our inventory list. Everybody had brought their rubber slingshots and as many ball bearing balls as they could find. We were good on this aspect, as I also had around half a bucketful of balls of different sizes obtained by breaking up several dozens of ball bearings I had carried from Vlădeni around the start of summer, when I visited that place. I had found the ball bearings thrown in the rubbish pit of the SMT[12] and, look, it had been a good thing I'd curved my backbone carrying them here. Some of us had bows and we decided to insert small nails in the tips of the arrows, because pieces of reed could not inflict much damage. For hand to hand arms, we also had a kind of spear made of large pieces of cast-off firewood, of which the first level of our cellar was full.

12 SMT – *Stațiunea de Mașini și Tractoare*, the Machines and Tractor Pool, usually attached to a cooperative farm.

But fighting the brave and numerous Red Army only with hand to hand arms did not sound too good, so we started to rack our minds for ideas regarding the improvement of our army's weapons. After a brainstorming session which I barely controlled – of course I did not know what it was back then, or how it was done – two good ideas took shape, which we eventually approved. It was even three ideas, if you don't consider Molotov cocktails with carbide and petrol as being versions of the same weapon, and yes, there was something I had tried before but had given up because my mother caught me and it didn't go easy on me, but we now had a case of force majeure, with the fatherland in danger. These were small cannon made of aluminium pipe from TV antennas, using as explosives either potassium chlorate mixed with sulphur, or the phosphorus prised off the heads of matches. We did not have potassium chlorate and sulphur, because there was a long time to go to the winter celebrations, nor did we have carbide, because there was still time, even up to St Parascheva's feast day[13], when we took great pleasure in disturbing the masses and the pilgrims. There was a canister of petrol in the cellar, and a multitude of empty bottles which I had not gotten around to selling[14]. Everybody was going to bring more bottles, and the petrol was going to be taken care of by Vlăduț and Nelu, because their fathers were drivers. We could get hold of carbide from the building site at *Casa Modei* fashion store nearby, and I appointed Moni and Dănuț to take care of this. There was still the potassium chlorate and the sulphur. As this was the holiday and the Russians could have

13   The relics of St Parascheva (or Paraskevi) are placed in Iași Metropolitan Orthodox Cathedral, attracting huge crowds on the saint's feast day of 14 October.

14   Bottles and glass jars could be sold to special collection centres; this was a normal way for children to make pocket money.

27

attacked us any day, if not any hour henceforth, we could not talk about stealing from the schools' chemistry labs, as we did before Christmas. In the end, we decided to obtain it by paying, not directly in cash, but in cigarettes instead, because all the schools' watchmen used to smoke. I knew the man from my lyceum. I had given him cigarettes before so he would allow us to play football on the school playground. Mircea and Țucu – God rest the latter, since he departed this world some years after the Revolution, knew the watchmen from the comprehensive school nearby, where they were actually enrolled. We could not just give them *Carpați*, so we had a little argument on choosing between *Litoral* and *Snagov*. *Litoral* was only 5 Lei, *Snagov* was 8, but it had a filter made of camel hair, according to the urban legend doing the rounds back then. We settled on *Snagov* and started to rifle through our pockets, but we only found money for one pack and a half. It was settled that I would fund the difference from my mother, as she had just returned very well disposed from Bucharest! We didn't have to tell the watchmen for what we needed the substances. We could not know if they were the Russians' spies or just some big-mouths, so we composed a story about a saint's feast somewhere in the countryside where we wanted to have fun at the expense of the faithful. Everything was settled, everyone had a task to achieve, and we were to see each other again at 14.00 hours. It was just the carbide that had still to be procured in the evening by Dănuț and Moni, after the builders left the site and there was only one watchman left there, who would get drunk in less than an hour and then go to sleep in a storeroom made of sheet-metal. Of course, we could have also bribed the man with a quarter-litre of "two blue eyes"[15], but that would have been a

---

15 "Two blue eyes" was the popular name for a cheap plum brandy featuring two blue plums on the label.

pity with regard to the money spent, which, in any case, we no longer possessed!

At 14.00 sharp, almost all of us were again in front of the cellar door. We went in. Taking the inventory, we now had two more petrol canisters, tens of empty bottles just perfect to be transformed into grenades, and the chlorate and sulphur procured by me. Mircea and Țucu were due to meet the comprehensive school watchman later on in the evening, because the director and some teachers were there on some business when they'd first visited. They had been smart enough not to give the cigarettes in advance. I had managed things pretty well, having a little more than 100 grams of each substance in two little jars, but I also had the impression the watchman wanted to get me talking, mentioning two Russian tanks destroyed overnight on the Ungheni Bridge, melted somehow by a new weapon which we alone, the Romanians, possessed. It was a weapon using light or something like that! But the watchman couldn't fool me! On the occasion of the liquidation of the *local government* districts and the *local government* sanitary directorates, my father – who had been left jobless – had been transferred to the hospital in Ungheni. He took me there on the train a couple of times, a trip some 20-minute long, and I had seen with my own eyes that there was no road-bridge there, only a railway crossing, a situation which stayed unchanged from then until the beginning of the 1990s, when the rail bridge acquired a sort of brother made of flowers![16] And now we don't have even that one!

---

16 *"Podul de flori"*, literally translated as the Bridge of Flowers, is the name of two events (on 6 May 1990 and 16 June 1991) when the people living on the two sides of the Prut river, the natural border between Romania and the Republic of Moldova, crossed the border freely into the others' country, without papers, for the first time since WW2 (and the establishment of the Republic, formerly part of the Kingdom of Romania). Vast amounts of flowers were thrown into the river on both occasions.

We were now well stocked with regard to fire weapons too! In the evening we were going to add to the arsenal other quantities of potassium chlorate and sulphur, plus the carbide! But we could start getting ready. On a piece of plank, I mixed thoroughly two parts chlorate and one part sulphur and sealed the mixture well in two little jars. We then searched the detritus in the cellars for some more robust pieces of plank and we built five gun carriages for the cannon, because we'd only managed to find five appropriate pieces of aluminium pipe in the storerooms of our houses. We flattened one end of each pipe with the hammer and tied them crosswise to the gun carriages by fixing them with some nails. We then started to fill the bottles with petrol, adding pebbles, sand and smaller metal balls which would fit down the bottlenecks. For wick fuses, we used thin nylon stockings, which we stabilised with pieces of "squeak" – that white and porous material that started to be used for the physical protection of merchandise[17], which we would rub on pieces of glass until we drove the grown-ups out of their minds. Around four o'clock we heard Cellu's grandmother calling him in, and I told him to leave slowly in order not to be noticed by anyone, and also not to say anything to anyone. We could trust him. One year previously, when the Six Day War was going on, he told us all that he was convincing his parents to go to Israel in order to fight with the Arabs man-to-man, and these latter were more numerous by I don't know how many times. This war with the Russians was just fine for him, he was getting a little training, and the Russians were also more numerous! We started to improve our hand to hand weapons by inserting small nails in the arrows' tips and big, 18-20 centimetre long nails in

17 Polystyrene.

the tips of the spears. In the meantime, I went up into the house a couple of times: on the one hand in order not to be looked for by my parents and so be caught in the middle of the arms race, and on the other hand in order to find out whether the Russians had already entered the country, forcing us to start the battle before the completion of the campaign preparations. No, they had still not entered. The TV played scenes from Czechoslovakia, the communiqué from the Party, sequences from Daddy's discourse of the previous day – they were only talking about the invasion anyway. There were also short interviews with people on the street and in factories, who were showing their solidarity with the Czechoslovak people, their support for the policy of the Party and their decision to join the patriotic guards. I was experiencing the satisfaction of having already built a kind of patriotic guard while the grown-ups were just getting prepared!

Well, everything that could have been done by that time was done, and well done at that! We thought that we should also try the firearms, our cannon, before going out in order to train with the hand to hand arms, so we wouldn't have unpleasant surprises in full battle mode. We knew the petrol bottles worked, as we hadn't made them any different from the other times when we had fought with the gang of Cloşca Street for the control of the football alley; but it was only me who had tried the cannon before, after I'd seen the model in Vlădeni. Where could we try them out, though, to see if they worked? Not outside, it was not possible, everyone would have heard it and gotten scared, believing the Russians were already upon us. We would also have gotten a ticking off, if not a beating from the grown-ups. The first level of the cellar was too close to the surface and you could have heard the noise almost as well as from the outside. The second level was again too high, and the sounds would not have been muffled enough. We could only descend to the lowest level, at the end of some fifty steps and a corridor which was some ten metres long. But the electricity hadn't worked down there for a while. Father kept on calling a specialist to fix it and the man kept on failing to appear. We would be at a depth of some fifteen metres, beyond the house, and somehow beyond the boulevard, under a kind of worn-out park which, although located in the centre of the city, would have probably been empty at that hour. Those who had flashlights in their homes were sent to get them, and in about ten minutes we had six flashlights with good batteries, which gave off a pretty good light by cumulative effect. We took the aluminium cannon and the jars with the explosive mix, some boxes with sand, pebbles and balls of the smallest kind, and we descended the stairs breaking the darkness with the beams of our flashlights. At the bottom there was a big, square room with sides some ten-twelve metres wide, from which started off two lateral galleries which were some two metres wide and five-six metres long. On the right hand-side there was a door blocked with stones and tied with wire, through which you could have entered the neighbouring cellar. Back then, before the foundations of the blocks of flats penetrated through, almost the entire city was undercrossed by such cellars, subterraneous corridors, and tunnels that communicated with each other, forming a vast network. I had actually tried to unblock the door to the neighbouring cellar once but I couldn't make it, it was too solidly barricaded. But I had seen what was on the other side during an exploration I took together with Nelu, who had managed to sneak the key away from the more aged neighbours in the house next to ours. It was not a cellar like our own because it was slightly narrower, less well compartmentalised, but I would have liked to add it to my vast subterraneous terrains.

I placed the first cannon in the gallery on the right, the pipe pointing at the inside, towards the wall at the end of the big room, thinking that we would take shelter on the sides of the entrance to the gallery. In principle, nothing wrong could happen to us, as we were protected by the enormous stone walls. I introduced into the aluminium pipe first the explosive mix, then two or three centimetres of sand and pebbles, then a couple of balls, then again some two centimetres of sand with pebbles. I'd placed at the root of the pipe a little tray made of the lid from a box for boiling syringes, which was filled with petrol. When everybody was sheltered behind the stone walls, I lit the petrol and ran to shelter myself as well. Time passed, but nothing happened! This is how time flies when you wait impatiently for something, but we thought that maybe the petrol was extinguished. We stayed motionless for a little while then we had a council and decided that somebody needed to take a look. Nelu looked at it and it seemed to him that the petrol was indeed off, or maybe it had run out before taking effect. Anyway, I decided to go and take a look. It was not for nothing that I was a commander of hosts. I went in and, because I heard others coming behind me, I turned to them to tell them to retreat. And then the boom was heard! I thought the house was going to fall on us. I felt a burn on my shoulder, but fortunately it was just from the flame and sand, as my mother was going to find out a little while later. For a change, Nelu was screaming with his hands on his face, and blood poured in rivers from under his palms. Mircea was looking, somehow hypnotised, at his left hand from where a piece of finger seemed to be missing, but blood gushed forth from his hand as if from a spring, too. We were hurt, stupefied, and almost deaf when my mother, father and sister barged in. By all appearances, the cannon pipe had also exploded at the same time as the substances, since Nelu had a piece of aluminium – a piece of shrapnel – stuck above his left eye, where a scar of which he was very proud was going to stay forever. It was a consequence of the war with the Russians! Mircea had lost the tip of his ring finger on the left hand, and I, who had been the closest, but fortunately with my back turned, had a pretty ugly wound on my left shoulder. It was not something deep, because there were no scars left except some sort of small, almost invisible white dots which always stay un-tanned, no matter how long they are exposed to the sun. Of course, I was going to find out about all this later on. For the time being I could not even comprehend how I'd ended up inside the house, where my mother and father cared for my wound, and I explained to them the noble circumstances in which I had received it. I do not remember much, not even if they gave me a beating, although I don't think they were in the mood to beat me. I was not just hurt, but also scared at the thought that the explosion could have caught me before I turned my face away.

I also remember a phrase said by my father in order to distract my attention while he painted me with iodised alcohol, or maybe his thoughts had simply became jumbled:

"These damned Russians, they make victims whether they invade you, or whether they don't!". I think he knew what he was saying, he had been an aviator during the war, in fact an on-board radio operator, and he had just begun teaching me the Morse code at the time of the expected invasion. On the screen of the TV images of Czechs were displayed, dead or arrested during the invasion, and long-haired youths were throwing at tanks stones which they had prised off the pavement…

2-5 February 2009

The Day Father Started to Die

They are different from us, those other people, all those other people, who start to die immediately after they are born, if not some nine months prior to that. My father started to die precisely on 19 May 2005, at 14 hours and 55 minutes, less than one month after we'd celebrated his 82nd anniversary. We were also celebrating mine, which was shorter than his by precisely three decades.

I was in the train station; there were still six minutes to the departure of the train for Cluj-Napoca, where I was going for a book launch coupled with a debate on extremism, and the director of the publishing house who was going to accompany me had not yet arrived. Agitatedly, I moved near the coach where we had our places, taking out my mobile to see what was going on, and it rang while I was getting ready to dial or locate the number. It was my sister, and she gave me the news: generalised cancer, starting in the right lung, with metastasis of the aorta, liver, and several of the other organs around, with the life expectancy of a few weeks, they didn't know how many. She told this to me brusquely, without any sort of preparation. That is the time when father started to die, on 19 May 2005, at 14 hours and 55 minutes – not from the moment of his birth onwards, not from some year previously when they had made the diagnosis of prostate cancer, and he had reacted favourably to the treatment. My sister admonished me for leaving in that precise moment, in those circumstances. Nevertheless I knew I had to leave. Not because, as I suspected, nothing could be done anymore, not because I wanted to keep my word to the organisers of the events to which I was invited, but purely and simply because I had to leave, to be able to receive this item of news calmly, alone. To be able to assimilate it, to interiorise it, to accept it, but how the devil could I have achieved such a thing, how could I have accepted that I was going to be an orphan on my father's side in a matter of weeks? Because the name of the father is the son, and the name of the son is that of the father. So my father started to die at that moment. Up to that moment, he had been, like all of us, an immortal. I had to be alone for this process of understanding and acceptance. I climbed inside the coach, sat on the seat at the window and prayed for my travelling companion to miss the train. She did not miss it, but she arrived only some seconds before the train's departure. I told her, just as brusquely as my sister had done, what was happening to me and she showed extraordinary tact by delving into the reading of a manuscript, leaving me to my own fate for the entire almost ten hours' duration of the road. When I asked her something – banal, concise matters connected to the book launch – she replied in an equally concise manner and carried on about her own business.

Heidegger believes that man is existence on the way to death, which to me seems to be an immense stupidity. In fact, man is immortal and stays like that until the moment when he starts dying. If things were otherwise, nobody would die a "natural death" anymore, from illness or accidents, because we would all choose voluntary death. Death is just the consciousness of death and, until it infuses us, we are all immortal. We are not born with the consciousness of death, but we learn it, we find out about it from others, because

– and Sartre is right here – hell is other people. Of course, nobody told father what diagnosis he had received, we left him with his thoughts about intercostal aches caused by age and rheumatism, but the consciousness of death – he received from us. At that time, in those two last weeks. Not by a rational route, not by running the old syllogism: "All men are mortal. I am a man. So I am mortal", but purely and simply by our means, by our behaviour, to speak frankly, by our great attention and the special care which we gave him in those two last weeks. Whatever he had desired, he would have received. Any whim would have been fulfilled, although he wished for almost nothing. And it was normal for us to behave like that, it was "human" to proceed like this! But this could not stop him from thinking. It was impossible not to demand an explanation for the fact that his son, who came to see him in the best of cases once a month on a quick visit, suddenly appeared almost every day and had the time to sit by his side, to invent interesting subjects connected with the daily occurrences, politics, prices, events. Or the fact that his beloved grand-daughter, together with her husband and the ten-month-old great-grandson crossed the Ocean tempestuously, just because they had been caught out by longing. Indeed, the trip had been planned beforehand and had to be a surprise about which I was the only one who knew. It was a surprise and I am glad it took place, when I remember the first and last meeting he had with this great-grandson, the appetite for play which I had seen only when his grand-daughter had been a child in her turn, and especially his last words, those before the departure, which my mother told me. Yes, we filled his two last weeks, we tried to bring him "an easy death", but I have no idea if this was what he desired. Maybe, instead of an easy death, he would have preferred an unexpected, unprepared one, unannounced by the consciousness of the end, which could not be otherwise but painful, heartrending, irrespective of how many and whatever the type of postures he assumed. As always, since I first met him, he had never let anything transpire of his possible anxieties, not even something of his physical suffering. Perhaps it was not very great? I do not know. I only know he stayed on the first analgesic from the beginning to the end, that he didn't have to progress to morphine, that he was conscious all the time, that he didn't need the bedpan and that he had the ambition to go by his own strength to the toilet for as many times he had needed it. But I do not know one thing of the night hours, when we were all sleeping and maybe he was not, about his thoughts of those times, and I don't even think I have the strength to imagine them. I prefer to remember events from the times he was immortal…

The oldest of them, I think the oldest memory is connected to a time when I was sick with measles, a fabulous winter with enormous snows, the sort that no longer exist now. I don't recall many details of the period of sickness itself, besides the fact that I had a fever and that "the illness smelled". I don't know precisely what I understood by this, but that smell of sickness, which I can remember even now, I feel it – somewhere in my nostrils or in the bottom of my lungs, irrespective of how much cigarette smoke has passed through them in the meantime. But I do not remember this event because of that smell, but because of the contrast with another smell that succeeded it, a cold, fresh, reviving smell. I was probably convalescing when father took me out to get some air and, even before seeing the snow, before feeling the cold, upon opening the door, my nostrils were struck by that smell which was alive, "healthy", fresh, which emphasised the wet, warm, old, "diseased" smell which I was going to leave behind. The snow was very high and there was a frost which I felt through my clothes and the soft blanket in which he had wrapped me. He took me walking on little paths made in the snow between the house and the neighbouring medical dispensary, where he and mother were working. He was talking to me, and I wasn't really replying because I was completely overcame by the illness that was coming to an end. I don't know how old I was. Of course, I could find this either from mother, because mothers remember almost everything, or by looking in the files with old papers, because they had kept almost the entire archive – even old payslips, from which, to my surprise, I found out that the salaries during the days of my first childhood were worth a few hundred Lei, since, with these new Lei, the majority have ended up to be the same nowadays! It is not important what age I had, however, but only the fact that this was the oldest memory of an event that probably brought me the awareness of smell, and probably also the awareness of contrasts. Yet, it is not my oldest memory, but only the oldest one of him. The one which is truly the oldest memory is, in fact, of his father – my grandfather's death, and it comes from summertime. Of course it is previous to the episode with the measles and the walk through the great snows of yore. So, it was summer and it was very hot, grandfather was laid out stiffly, in city clothes, on the table, in the coffin, and a fly kept on landing on his face. I remember his face perfectly, exactly like in the only photograph of him that still exists, one with the dimensions of pictures for identity cards, and I also remember the fly. I do not remember any other face, although I remember a multitude of people, who have no face, they have rubbed-out faces, like they do now on television when the producers are being careful not to identify someone. Only the faces of grandfather Andrei and Marghioala, the woman who took care of the house, who kept on chasing away the fly, which always landed on grandfather's forehead, nose and cheek. I wanted to write a novel about him, about his adventures, even in my teenage years: *The Life and Deeds of Anton Andrei in Europe and America*, but I have not even managed to start on it. Nevertheless, he had a death on a par with his adventurous life.

I do not remember this, in fact; I know it from family stories. He thought he was gravely ill and mother and father checked him up and calmed him down in vain, because he wanted a medical check-up with a doctor "from the town". One summer's day, when he went to the county centre in his cart in order to bring medication for the dispensary, father took grandfather with him. He took him to a great number of doctors and found out, of course, that there was nothing grave, that his health was enviable. As the good news had to be celebrated, they went to a boozer at the town's exit and they partied so well that grandfather claimed the right to drive the horses himself, especially since the driver provided little resistance and had fallen asleep among the sacks and boxes of medication. He drove like the wind, in tune with his disposition, and the cart fell into a ditch on the side of the highway with the sacks and boxes of medication on top of them. Besides grandfather, nothing wrong befell either the people or the animals, but he was crushed by the edge of the cart's basket. He lived two more days, nothing could be done. I could say that, although pretty old, he died as fit as a fiddle! Although he never said this, I think father could not forgive himself for not stopping him from climbing into the cart's steering, and for not reining him in better, since he'd let him loose to drive the horses. Grandmother, with whom I talked a lot during my childhood and who taught me to read and write when I was around four or five years old, reproached herself for nothing. She gave me enough proofs that nobody and nothing could stop grandfather when he had something on his mind.

In fact, I lie – or I forgot: I did write some pages about grandfather Andrei and his Swiss cows. I made a very summary sketch of his life in a book about intellectuals.

A memory from my childhood. In fact, a reconstruction, because I do not remember almost anything directly, but I appealed to other people's memories, those of my parents', as well as to the memories culled from the stories constructed out of my grandmother's memories. Grandfather Andrei, a native of Bukovina, nicknamed towards the end of life "Burduşilă" [18] – et pour cause! [19] –, *did not own too much land in his native mountain village, so he descended to Moldavia, to Santa Mare, somewhere near Botoşani, and got hired as some sort of steward on an estate that stretched for thousands of hectares on both sides of River Prut. It appears that grandmother was a very beautiful woman in her youth, and the landowner's heels were hot for her, so much so that, in the end, grandfather had to fire some shots*

---

18 Loosely translated either as Stuffed-Face or Bruiser, depending on the original meaning of the verb "*a burduşi*", which can mean either to stuff (including one's face) or to give a sound beating.

19 *And for good reason*. In French, in the original.

in his direction in order to cool him down. He didn't hit him. Maybe he was too angry, maybe he didn't even want to hit him, because he was a good marksman, as grandmother used to tell it. But he had to flee, and he ran so much that he only stopped when he got to a mine in California. He didn't calm down there, either. He imagined that his business there was not just to extract ore from the mine, but also to "plot" at the unionisation of the miners. He was deported for the first time. He returned to the home country and gave grandmother her second child, the first one being born a little while before his departure. He left again for America, but this time to Canada, somewhere near Montréal. Again on unionising business. He was again deported. He gave grandmother another child and left again. This happened some five or six times. There's just one thing that worries me: wouldn't it have been better to take grandmother with him? Father would have been born there and I would now be the descendant of an American citizen. As things are, going in roundabout manner, I am only the grandfather of Andrew, who bears his name, just like Andreea who also bears his name in the feminine version, with Andrew being an American citizen by birth. What is certain is that, although being a sort of commuter between America and Europe and more of an anarcho-syndicalist than a dim-witted miner, grandfather still managed to amass a small fortune. When he decided to stay in the country for good, he bought a herd of Swiss cows, the most renowned at that time. He managed to save them from the successive requisitions of the Romanians, the Germans and then of the Russians, hiding them in the woods, so that, at the end of the war, the herd was even bigger than it had been to begin with. So he was an established householder when the communists decided the time for the "socialisation of agriculture" had come. The first thing that he lost was precisely the herd of cows. He did not oppose it. He was old, he had already stopped owning a gun for some years, the children were in schools or working for the state, but those who opposed it were, mysteriously, the cows. Less than one month from being confiscated, after their entrance into the collective household, as they used to say back then, the cows began no longer to produce twelve-fifteen litres of milk daily, but only two or three saucers-full. They were anti-Communist cows it seems. They did not get accustomed in any way to the collectivist stables. The new leaders of the village called meeting after meeting, but they did not manage to convince the cows to become productive again. Not even the Party inspector from the county centre, or not even the regional inspector, managed to do it. Not even the man from the Securitate secret police, who was in charge of the village, could manage it. This latter tried the hardest, screamed at them and threatened them with his handgun. In the end, he proposed moving grandfather's cows to a separate stable, which does smell like factionalism – and it was a quite a wonder he was not kicked out from the Securitate services of his mother's [20]! But the cows – nothing! In the end they were slaughtered, so that my grandfather's co-villagers, who were not allowed to slaughter their own animals because they were given up as quotas, ate their fill of meat for a good period of time. We could say that the cows chose suicide rather than slavery. When I was a child, I would ask grandmother: well, if the cows didn't want to give milk to the CAP collective farm, why didn't they give them back to grandfather? Grandmother would laugh and say to father: this child has more mind than all these communists taken together. In fact, we were both wrong, both me and grandmother: the logic of

---

20 A very Romanian way of swearing at somebody, without making use of rude words, is to mention their mother's ownership of something completely unrelated.

*the system was a completely different one, but I was going to find
this out much later…*

Memories. There are many memories, a multitude of
them gathered in an already semi-centennial life, and it is
even a little more than a semi-centenary since we had the
chance to be here together. Me and my father. My father and
I. There was a period of time around the end of lyceum and
the beginning of the university which I did not understand
back then, and I still do not understand now. Father never
was a chatty man, you could sit even for a whole day with
him without exchanging one sentence. For a change, we
understood each other by signs and gazes, but during that
period he was really silent, very silent. He almost did not
talk, except completely functionally, and only if he had
no choice. During that period, he would prop himself for
hours on end at the window of the house's entrance door
and he would gaze somewhere into a void. I did not know
what he was thinking about, whether he was thinking of
anything, nor what exactly was he seeing. In the end, from
that window he could not see anything apart from some old
Jewish houses, like ours, all lost in the great earthquake of
1977. He didn't say anything about his taciturn experiences,
or about what he was contemplating. It did not even pass
through my head, not even later on, to ask him about that
period, about that experience which always seemed to be
important and now looks fabulous precisely because it can
no longer be recovered. I regret that we did not do it at least
in our last month together. It would be indecent to try and
invent or to make suppositions, but I am convinced that I
lost something important from his life by not asking those
questions at least in those last days, in the last moments. But

if he had not spoken, I would also continue to feel blocked. I always thought he was a very severe man, although there were signs that this was not the case, that I had not found the access route. At family parties, after two-three glasses of wine, he didn't just talk, but he also told jokes, displaying a personality different from the majority of the guests, stuffed shirts whose conventional manners shielded them from the possibility of telling blue jokes. He even sang. In comparison with me, since I had lost my voice when it was breaking, he had a singing voice, a very full and warm tone -baritone going to bass - and I even wonder if, during some period of his life, he had trained it. There was only one uncle, the husband of a sister of my mother's, who is now very old and very ill, and who had a better, more exercised, but higher voice, that of a tenor. When his grand-daughter was born and I saw how he used to spend time with her, how he invented games and stories, how he went on all fours so that she could climb and ride on him, I realised that I had lost out on a part of the joys of childhood. On the other hand it would not have even crossed my mind that I could dare such a thing. Maybe I would not even have been allowed it, as grandparents are more indulgent with their grandchildren than with their children, anyway. The feeling, however, that I had lost something, that I had lost out on something else, stayed with me and is still haunting me. I am haunted even more by the thought that I was not able to find out anything about those long states of gazing into a void, of contemplation. I see him very precisely, leaning on the entrance door, silent, looking towards somewhere, to something. If you wanted to enter or exit the door, he would step aside gently, then he returned to that somewhat relaxed position. He would smoke, sometimes. At other times he would stay for hours on end without even smoking. He – who until reaching pensionable age, would smoke three packs of *Carpați* every day, then only ten cigarettes, and then he gave up smoking completely around the age of seventy, when he had a crystalline lens replacement surgery and was immobilised in bed for almost one week.

He was not just silent, but also improbably calm. I don't think I have seen him angry more than ten times during this long period of life. He never shouted at me, nor at the others, from what I saw. He did not admonish me either, instead he would draw my attention very quietly to something when it seemed necessary to him, and this only if the naughty things I did were wholly "remarkable". It is incredible how much freedom to move I had during my entire childhood and adolescence. He would not ask where I was going, or when I was coming back, but I don't think I was overdoing this aspect of things. If I asked him for money – rarely, as I had learned to get around by selling empty bottles and jars – he would not ask what I needed it for. If I said to him that I wanted to go to the films or a show, he put his hand in the pocket on the right hand side of the trousers, where he kept coins and small banknotes, and gave some to me without saying anything. If it was about a book, he would proffer a note worth ten and one worth twenty-five, and I would choose the most suitable one. He did not ask what the cost was, and he did not expect the rest back. He did beat me three times, but, again, in a calm, proper manner, with a belt, not exaggeratedly hard – a thing which annoyed me terribly each time. He beat me more out of principle rather than because he enjoyed doing it. I would have preferred him to scream at me, and not to control his blows. I think that would have seemed easier to endure. I probably deserved two beatings. The one during my middle childhood I still account as unjust even today. In the end, what had I done? I used to collect anything in my childhood: stamps, coins, photographs of actors and footballers from the packs of chewing gum brought from Denmark, other photos of actors which were sold in cinemas, almost anything. Naturally, there also came the time for keys. When one day he saw the strings of keys which I had collected, some of them old, even antiques, some of them new, I don't know why he imagined I wanted to become a housebreaker, a thing which did not even cross my mind! Very calmly, in a methodical and reserved manner, he administered my second beating. The first one, I deserved – according to the rules of society back then, but not to those of society nowadays, which is founded on free initiative. I had started to run, for some months, a black market in cinema tickets. Since we were during the times of the minor communist liberalisation, there were a lot of capitalist films coming our way, with Alain Delon, Jean Marais, Gina Lollobrigida, Sophia Loren and so on. I had learned by heart the dialogue in the film *Cartouche*, with Belmondo and Lollobrigida, which I had seen some ten times. Everybody went to the films, but they did not have the time to buy tickets, so I would wake up around seven and when they opened the box office I would buy ten or more tickets for the afternoon shows, those starting at five or seven, which were in demand. I would sell the tickets worth two Lei for eight or even ten Lei, even for a film like *Romulus and Remus*. To somebody from Galați, who had missed the film in that town, I sold a ticket for 20 Lei. I had learned to negotiate, to feign that I could not give up going to the film and other tricks. I had the makings of a capitalist! I would make some good tens of Lei, sometimes even over one hundred a day, which I would spend almost as easily as they had been gained. I would take the other kids to the cake shop, we would buy cigarettes and smoke them in hiding, and I gave a good part of it to the beggars, the centre of the town being full of them. When business was done, on the road from the cinema to the Metropolitan Cathedral, where we lived at the time, some half of the money went to the beggars, which made me feel like some kind of *haiduc* brigand who takes from the rich and gives to the poor. My activity as a free entrepreneur lasted for a few months, until somebody squealed on me, or maybe father himself saw me by chance. Anyway, one day when I was running tight negotiations for the sale of a ticket, I felt myself caught by a hand, somehow from behind. I thought it was some militiaman who I had not managed to suss out in the crowd, and I was scared. But I was even more scared when I saw it was father. He only said "come", slowly and calmly, and I accompanied him home. Once there, as calm as before, he administered the first beating. I remember it well. I deem it authorised, even if it definitively annulled my spirit of free economic initiative. It is clear. I will never become either a player at the stock exchange, or a speculator on the real estate market!

The third beating was because of sandals. They had bought me new sandals, because I had to go to summer camp at the seaside, and they had been stolen from me at the lido. In principle, I was probably not even supposed to know where the lido was, because they had never taken me there, and I was already swimming very well. I liked it and

I forgot to come out of the water again. I wouldn't buy a ticket, but I would jump over the fence, which meant that I couldn't deposit my clothes in the cloakroom, but I left them on the sand, usually near somebody's sheet, asking them to pay attention to my clothes as well – which, in the end, were short trousers, a shirt and some sandals. This time the sandals were new, bought that morning, so they had become attractive and I didn't find them when I finally came out of the pool. I wandered through the town, barefoot, until it was evening. I prepared a story about some boys who had proposed a speed contest in tree climbing, and I reached home late. Barefoot. I had not even managed to finish the story, when father took out his belt, placed my head between his knees, applied some blows and announced that the next morning I would leave for camp in my old, almost broken sandals. There was no other store open. The second day, around five in the morning, we left together on foot for the train station, which was some hundreds of metres' distance from the house, then on the train to the coast. He did not utter a word in front of me, although he emitted monosyllables towards the other children in the group, and I took pains to keep my feet under the bench so that nobody would see the old scraps I had on my feet. But he was not cruel to the end. He bought a pair of new sandals from a store which was very near the station in Eforie Sud, at the seaside, advising me to keep the others as well, the old ones, because you can never know what contests I would take part in again. Yes, he would talk rarely, but always with a certain irony, and, most of the time, his silent stares were also somewhat ironic.

He knew I was busy with writing, even in my primary

school, when I would write my "novels" of partisans and Germans, or about cowboys, but I don't think he'd read anything until very much later on. I shall invoke the episode of the first texts which he had certainly read, but I now remember that, when I was about halfway through my lyceum studies, he gave me a typewriter. A black, old, portable machine, with a box which was also black, made of wood, covered in a strong and shiny paper. On a small metal plate fixed in screws on the wooden box was written: "Cartea Românească Publishing House, Bucharest, King Carol I Boulevard…" That had probably been the first, pre-war, owner, and who knows what route it had taken to enter the ownership of the cooperative where father had ended up as an accountant after the disestablishment of the old counties and regions – so, it was around 1966. The machine had been sent for scrap because of its age, and because they had received typewriters which were new, GDR-made [21] and shiny. Father took it to be fixed and oiled and gave it to me. I think it was the most important gift he ever gave me. I typed on that machine until the last year in university, when my parents, being already completely convinced that my fate was definitively tied to writing, gave me Miss "Erika", a new typewriter, GDR-made, of course, which was to accompany me until 1990, when I switched to an orange electric typewriter, received from "humanitarian aid" – in fact, from somebody from Radio "Free Europe" who had interviewed me. Starting in 2000, I too got modernised. I switched to the computer. All those typewriters still exist: the "Continental" and "Erika" are in their house, although he is no longer there – I can't refer to that house as being only

---

21 GDR – the German Democratic Republic, or the German Communist state, a source of German technology for the entire Eastern Bloc.

mother's! – and the electrical one is here, near me, behind me in fact, where I am now, seated at the desk, writing this story on the computer.

The summer I entered university I had my first, or maybe even my only, longer discussion with him. A serious discussion, as from father to son, or even from man to man. I was rid of the admission exam and he had procured a job for me for a month: to count the trees on the lower part of the town and to measure the hedges with a sort of divider, so that I would gather some good money for the holiday at the seaside. One afternoon when I returned feeling pretty hazy from the sun and all the walking, he said he wanted to discuss something with me and he started slowly towards the door. I started after him, but we did not go far, merely some tens of metres, up to Tosca, the closest bar, where sometimes both I and he entered, but, until that time, never together. I had drunk in front of him before, but only for the events in the family. I was wary even about smoking in front of him or mother, although they knew about it. Once, when I was still in the lyceum, when I was going to school in the morning, I put my hand in the jacket pocket looking for the small pack of Diplomat, with twelve cigarettes, and I did not find it. I found instead a three-Lei coin, the cost of the packet. He probably had not managed to get cigarettes and he had self-serviced, but with payment! So we entered the Tosca and he asked me what I wanted to drink. I replied somewhat provocatively that I wanted a Pinot Gris de Coteşti, a wine I had discovered at the previous New Year party, spent in Bucharest with my best cousins. I thought they would not stock something like it in that place, but they had it and they brought a bottle. For him, we ordered a Pilsner beer, Czech-made – in 1972 you could still find it freely available, and I knew it was his favourite beer. The waiter filled our glasses, and we started to drink in silence. We stayed silent like that for some quarter of an hour, maybe more, until the moment when, almost without breathing, he said to me the longest phrase I had ever heard coming from his mouth. I do not remember it exactly, although maybe I should have retained it because of the eloquence of his performance! Anyway, he was congratulating me for the high average grade with which I had entered the School of Sociology. He also said that he knew I was very smart, and that, if I proposed something to myself in a serious manner, I would succeed. He knew also that he had not intruded in my choices because each bird in her tongue singeth or dieth[22]. Well, in the end, if I wanted to make a career in the direction I had chosen, I had to join the Communist Party! With the last thing he blew me down! He had not joined it. What's more, he often crafted ironies aimed at mother, who had joined "for the children", telling her that she was the leading force of the family. I reminded him of all this, and he replied he had not joined because he was not interested in a career, but only in the family, to see us grown up and so on and so forth. I said to him I did not want a career either, that I was a writer, that I did the Sociology exams because I was in love with a girl who was doing her exams there, and that was why I had learned like crazy and had given up the Medical School exam, for which I had prepared for some two years, not because I had a special passion for this field of study about which I did not even know a great deal. He did not insist, and we

---

22 Paraphrase after the proverb *Fiecare pasăre pre limba ei piere*, which could be interpreted as everything that happens to a person happens because of their deeds.

finished our bottles discussing superficially about how the tree counting went, about the time I was to leave for the seaside, and about nothings. But I was left with his question still in my head: "How do you know you are a writer?", so that, once we got home (me – slightly staggering, he – not at all), I entered my room and I took the two pages typed on the "Continental", the first essay in a never-finished book I had courageously titled *Phallic-clitoral Essays*. I took only the first essay, "About hasty absolutism", but did not include the flyleaf, or the one-page preface, and with the pages in my hand I went to their room and proffered them to him. While he read, I stood up without moving, glued to the corner of the table, in an attitude which was rather hostile, on the opposite side to that where he sat. He read:

The sentence "All men are mortal" is erroneous. Even more, it is tendentious and malevolent. How could I sign such an affirmation while I am alive? Only the last of the dead men can support this. What surprises me is the fact that not one of the great exegetists of the commonplace has found the necessary time for the destruction of such an aberration.

The error proceeds from the illegitimate extension of a finding referring to all cases up to a given moment, to the absolute totality of possible cases, something that proves a very cavalier sense of nuance and a disarming absence of the spirit of finesse. Furthermore, one is talking here about the imperialist tendency of the atheist and positivist spirit, which, observing of itself as being immortal believes that the Christian, Buddhist or Mohammedan ones also suffer from the same worrying lack of perfection.

The devastating effect of such an affirmation almost does not

55

even need to be revealed. *What can a man who knows himself to be a priori condemned to death look like? Look at his heavily ringed eyes, his hesitating walk and the forehead tormented by lines. Look at that youth with an athletic stature and a perfect appearance of an Ares or Hercules. How fearful when he crosses the road, how he hesitates before running after the tram. Can such a man take a decisive decision, dares he accomplish anything? Such a man is nought but fear and submission, the slave of slaves and the emperor of fools! And it is natural, then, for him not even to deserve his life, and it is as natural to cling to it by his teeth and to moan impotently!*

At first sight, it seems strange that not only the mediocre have fallen prey to such gross error, but also intelligent spirits, minds of the choicest provenance, such as Aristotle or the Marquise de Beauvoir, who even commits the imprudence of titling one of her novels precisely thus. Let us look at things with more attention. Let us take the infamous phrase and, absolutely haphazardly, the phrase saying that Socrates is a man. We shall obtain the two premises of a syllogistic figure whose conclusion maintains without the possibility of negation that "Socrates is mortal!", whose immense stupidity frightens me. But who could have found usefulness in such a conclusion? First of all, the stupid and the mediocre, of course, but, among others, also old Aristotle, who would have eliminated an adversary from the path to personal glory, forgetting the proverb about whoever digs a hole for the others. Lord, to which limits can envy and the thirst for grandeur push even the most chosen of immortals!

I watched him with great concentration as he read. It seemed clear to me that he liked it, that it amused him; he smiled from the left corner of the mouth, a physiognomic expression I inherited as well. When he finished, he nevertheless told me that my thesis was as illegitimately generalising as the one I was combatting, and that, even worse, I risked a dangerous overpopulation of the earth. I grew upset; I would have wished him only to say that he liked it, because I had clearly seen that he did. While he had said the above to me, he proffered the two pages – these two pages: because, yellowed as they are by the more than three decades that have passed, they are here, near the computer keyboard. So he proffered them back to me. I plucked, rather than took them. I went out of their room like a tornado, entered my own room and I wrote, without pausing, this "Addenda to 'About hasty absolutism'":

Those ideas affirmed in the prior essay could lead the innocent reader, and even the more experienced one, to the conclusion that the author of these lines is an adherent of the assertion "All men are immortal". But nothing can be more erroneous. Only a foolish, unknowing mind, maybe sick, would maintain in a serious manner an enormity which is damaging even to our fate on earth.

Let us imagine only such a world in which everyone, to the last village idiot, would know themselves to be immortal. What could it be otherwise than a boundless empire of laziness, vice and stupidity? Immense flocks of imbeciles, laying about one on top of the others, melted by alcohol, by debauchery, concupiscence and inactivity, exhaling unbearable stenches, exhibiting their sexes[23]. Brrr! Can't you feel how your hairs stand on end imagining these loathsome finites which are different in no manner from the slugs and rats we sometimes find in the cellars, or other places hidden from the light of sun, in old houses, in former store-rooms of the

23 Author's note: *"Wow, what an image!" (note by Luca Piţu in 1973 or 1974).*

57

Jewish shops in the Old Kingdom and even in the Empire? I shall spare you! I shall stop the description before you are obliged to burst into a run from your own habitats to such a place. I shall, thus, stop the disgusting tableau, offering a solution, the only one possible anyway, between two evils which are equally great and unforgiving.

If each of us should consider himself as he thinks fit – and here the rapport between the two fundamental instincts of man, Eros and Thanatos, is crucial – in conformity with a known theory, that of great numbers – and a number between three and fifteen billion, the population of the Earth at the end of the last world conflagration and that estimated for the year 2100, can be considered without any doubt as a great number – we shall naturally reach a tendency to equilibrium. An equilibrium between optimism and pessimism, between activism and passivism, between morality and immorality etc., which can ensure a satisfying evolution of our species.

It is understood by itself that my option between immortality and finite existence must take place absolutely freely, because it would take place in conformity with each person's power to create, each one being that which they can be. Any intervention of an external will in the choice made by a free will must be prohibited, as it would not do anything but complicate things uselessly, disturbing the natural tendency for equilibrium. I have described the horrifying results above. Take care!

Immediately after I tapped the key with the exclamation mark, I pulled the page from the typewriter and went to their room. He was lying on the bed, I think he had fallen asleep, but he opened his eyes when I heaved the door open and entered. I proffered the two freshly written pages and I sat down near him, on the side of the bed. He raised himself halfway, arranged his pillow and, again without saying a thing, read what I had brought. He finished. He looked at me and said: "Yes, Liviu, I think you blew it, you are a writer". I went pretty dazed out of the room. I don't know if he called me by my name ten times in this life, his appellatives varied from "*şmecherson*" – crafty son, and "young gentleman", but he called me by my name, each time, only in important moments. For example, in the autumn of 1989, when the Wall fell and we were both in tears listening to the radio, and he said: "You were right, Liviu, communism is over, it is over". Even if in our country it was going to last for another month, I was convinced that it was over. Also because of everything I was finding out about what was going on, of course, but also because he had said it to me, he – who talked so rarely and so little.

Why did I become a writer? Because I had talent? It is possible, but I am not very certain of this either. Because I learned how to write and read some two years before going to school? Because I started reading and writing novels when I was in the second year in school? Once again, it is possible. But all these were premises. I think I started to consider myself a writer because of that discussion when I was nineteen years of age, because of that short phrase he pronounced at the end of the reading of the second essay from my young days. I do not realise what exactly made him say that thing at the time, but I do know that I always behaved, afterwards, in conformity to those words. This is why it did not cease to preoccupy my mind, and to hurt me, that he did not assimilate my essay *ad litteram*; perhaps I would now be sitting down with him with a glass of Pinot Gris for me and Pilsner for him. Or perhaps he assimilated it, in a higher or deeper sense. Otherwise, he would not visit me almost every night before I fall asleep…

I wear his watches, which were left as inheritance. I wear them alternately, some days the Swiss one, whose history I do not know or remember, a golden watch with a strap of brown leather which I attached, instead of its white metallic bracelet which did not match it. Then, for some other days, I wear the Soviet watch, Pobeda, which he had bought with his first salary, worth some few hundreds of Lei, that he received from the dispensary near which I spent my childhood. Although the first one is obviously a quality watch, an expensive watch, I do not know why I prefer to wear the other one; maybe because it is his first watch. At some given moment I have also worn his wedding rings, the gold one from the marriage and the silver, anniversary one, but at some point it seemed improper, even in bad taste, so I now keep them in a little teak box on my desk. Some years ago I believed he visited me every night before I sank into sleep because I was wearing his watches, objects which he would not take off his hand either, before going to sleep, as if he had to know the exact time while sleeping – he, who never seemed to hurry, who was never late: and all this without even looking at the watch. But I was wrong: he still visited me. Even if I took the watches off; he is still visiting, and why shouldn't he do it? If he allowed me to be free – as far as it is possible to be free during one's childhood and adolescence – why should he be the one who deprived himself of this freedom? Perhaps this is also proof of the fact that the conclusions of the essays I wrote at the end of my adolescence were not wrong.

February 2007

In a Village, within the Szekler Area in Transylvania, the Holy Virgin's Icon, All of a Sudden, Started to Speak...

At the age of almost eighty years, Pastor Mathias did not really have memories from before the time he had started to serve in this village thrown over the hills between the forests in the Szekler lands[24]. These forests were otherwise becoming more and more sparse, year after year, because this is how times of transition are: rough and greedy. Yet even those memories he possessed were diffuse and slow-paced, life shaping itself according to a ritual which seemed as unchanging as the one he celebrated on Sundays, on feast days or on the occasion of crucial events in life: baptisms, weddings, funerals, and the various commemorations he observed alongside his parishioners. Other events, which I should call circumstantial, did not really come to his mind, although he had established his life there at the end of the war when he had finalised his studies at the seminary, and he had lived through the two great changes of recent history here.

The war? The second one, of course, because during the time of the first he had barely started to open his eyes to

---

24 The Szekler lands (*Ținutul Secuiesc* in Romanian or *Szekelyföld* in Hungarian) is an area of Romania covering counties Harghita and Covasna, and partially county Mureș, in eastern Transylvania. They are predominantly inhabited by Szeklers (*Secui* or *Székely*), a Hungarian population.

the world. He was born in an empire, but when he started to go to school he was already living in a kingdom of more modest dimensions, and all this without him even realising it.

He did not realise even when and how it was, that, besides the language spoken in the home, he started to speak the Romanian language, a thing which was useful after the war, when part of the Romanian families, unsettled by the disestablishment of the Uniate Church[25], came to his church. In the end, this is only natural; the life of a clergyman should not be moved by events that are as passing as the wind, but only directed by essential matters, which are always the same, and which have always been repeated again and again from the birth of the Saviour to this day, in every place where the faith in Resurrection has spread. I don't even know whether these were exactly his thoughts on that summer morning when, having woken up early, performed his ablutions and changed into new clothes, he exited his house slowly and started peacefully, meditatively and serenely towards the church of his life, which he knew by heart down to the minutest details.

I had only been in the village for some two days, having arrived from Sfîntu Gheorghe[26], where I had taken part in some kind of symposium, the likes of which were fashionable back then in the first years after the change and after the

---

25 The Uniate Church, also known as Greek or Eastern Catholic Church, represented a large religious community in Transylvania, whose faithful were largely ethnic Romanians under the religious guidance of the Pope, but following a ritual closely connected to that of the Greek Orthodox rites. The Uniate Church was disestablished and banned by the post-WW2 communist government in Romania, and its churches and properties confiscated.

26 Sfîntu Gheorghe is a municipality in the county of Covasna, and the capital of that county.

bloody events of Tîrgu Mureş[27], which was dedicated to intercultural, interfaith and interethnic relations. An older acquaintance of mine, who was among the organisers, had brought me here to see with my own eyes how the Hungarians, the majority population in the village, got along with the few tens of Romanian families with whom they had lived together since the world and the earth had been made, as my friend used to say, happy that she had converted so well into Romanian a formula they also often used in Hungarian – as she had told me almost immediately after I'd reached the symposium. She belonged to a mixed family, the minority of a minority, as one might say, the folks who are the most exposed in troubled times. Although her mother was Hungarian, she had a Romanian name of the most genuine kind – I think it was Zamfira, if, after so many years in which we have not seen each other, my memory still serves me more or less faithfully. So, I had been in the village for two days at the time, and I lived with the Romanian grandmother of Zamfira. It may be because of the change in locality or because of the excitement caused by my arrival into an unknown environment, but I had woken up at the crack of dawn, and after I drank my coffee I went walking on a new route through the village. I was going down a hill on which the Romanian side of the village was situated and, far in the distance, towards the other end, I saw the pastor slowly emerging from his house and taking the direction of the church in which he'd served for such a long and bitter time. (I used this latter form of words deliberately, as it is,

---

27   On 20 March 1990, groups of ethnic Romanians and Hungarians clashed in the city of Tîrgu Mureş in Transylvania in a short lived conflict that ended with 5 deaths and 278 wounded. The change alluded to earlier in the paragraph is the Romanian Revolution of December 1989, which deposed the dictator Nicolae Ceauşescu and his communist government.

63

once again, one of those which Zamfira was very proud of using.) Seeing the pastor, I too started at a leisurely pace towards the church, aiming to give him the time to solve whatever problems he had to solve inside, before the start of the church service. We had decided on the previous day to find a pause for a longer discussion, some sort of interview about his life here and about its events, although he had said it would have been more appropriate to talk about the lack of events. In that case, I agreed, it should be about non-events. We had established that we would talk after the mass, in which I wanted to participate, because he had told me he was holding it bilingually out of respect for the Romanian parishioners, although almost all of them understood the Hungarian language.

I was on the way, some tens of metres from church, when I saw Father Mathias emerging hurriedly from the holy building and somehow making his way towards me, although he evidently did not see me. He now seemed as unsettled, as he had been calm when I saw him going in. The hair, which, from the distance, had seemed to be nicely arranged, was now standing on its end; his coat was unbuttoned at the neck, and even his shirt was also unbuttoned. He was muttering something. When he passed by me, without noticing me, I heard him say: "It's speaking, the icon is speaking …". He then gained some distance and I stopped understanding any of his words clearly. I was surprised he was speaking Romanian, although, in moments of trouble, I think it is more natural to talk in your maternal language. I turned suddenly and I saw him going towards the edge of the forest on the hill neighbouring the one on which the Romanian side of the village was located. I sat on a bench near the church fence and I racked my brain in order to try and understand what had happened. The icon is speaking? So what is wrong with this, what is the reason for being troubled? One day previously, we had just joked together on the subject of the spectacular proliferation of holy icons that speak or cry, and other kinds of miracles like the crosses which woodcutters keep on finding imprinted in the heart of the tree when they split some log or an old tree stump. The country had been filled with miracles from the time of revolutionary change onwards, and I can't see why these miracles should have bypassed only the Szekler lands! He had met other villagers on the road to the edge of the woods, and he had also probably managed to unsettle them to some extent, since they were now coming nearer to the church one by one. They hesitated for a while in front of the door, then went inside and came out much more troubled than when they had gone in. Other folks, from other directions, were simply coming in order to take part in the mass, but they came out as troubled as the others. They all muttered something on exiting, but as I did not speak Hungarian I did not understand a thing. At some point, I understood something from a woman who, coming out of the door in a hurry, was saying – and she was saying this to herself – in Romanian: "Lord, what sins did we commit…" She then, in her turn, followed the tracks of the others, towards the edge of the woods, where they had all started to gather around the priest. Obviously the woman must have been very affected by what had happened to her in the little church – or maybe she was from one of the Romanian families who had converted to the Reformed confession. I was looking at those who entered and exited hurriedly from the church, anxiety written on their faces; I was also looking at the people who gathered around the priest, who seemed to have started the church service right there, at the edge of the woods, under the blue expanse of the skies – and I failed to understand a thing. I thought of everything that could have been more disastrous: perhaps some provocation or an act of profanation of the holy place had happened. And I can't say to this day if I had been right in my apprehensions.

I eventually mustered enough courage. Curiosity always vanquishes fear, and anxiety. I stood up from the little bench and made my way to the church. Even before I stepped over its threshold, I heard a warm, clear voice speaking from inside. I went in, making the sign of the cross. The icon of the Holy Virgin was speaking in Romanian. Our country might be the garden of the Mother of God, as Pope John Paul II had said when he visited us, but this was too much! I, too, left the church in a hurry, and much troubled. I went home to Zamfira's grandmother, found her there, and I can't recall what I said to her, but I was in the car with all my bags packed in a matter of minutes, on the road to the rail station in Sfîntu Gheorghe. I was on the train before lunchtime. Not the train home, but to Bucharest – which was the first one that came and went. In this type of situation, people are always looking for a guilty party and, as I had learnt, not so much from my own experience but from what I had read, the problem is not that folk are always looking for a scapegoat. The problem is that they always find one.

October 2010

The Second Confession of Maria, the Other Maria

The character Maria dedicates this confession to the real Sabina, the one who gave her the notebook

My name is Maria and I am trying, at my almost forty years of age, to find out what I'm all about. I am looking for myself and maybe I shall find myself. There are moments when I need to talk; I know I need to talk. I tried to – with my friends, with my girlfriends, but it did not work. Something blocked me, I could not get to the end of it, great chunks of truth stayed hidden. Not because we might have been talking about special, very grave, very unpleasant or very pleasant matters, but because a blockage appeared, purely and simply, a geological fault was gaping and I could no longer cross over it, I could no longer talk. Once, after reading an article in a popular magazine, I thought a psychotherapist might solve this. You noticed they started to appear in our country as well. And even to have a clientele, although people are not yet that rich in our little country. I chose a woman, thinking it would be easier for me, that I would be able to open up easier, but nothing happened. She was a lady in-between two ages, who wished herself livelier and more relaxed than her powers could allow her to be, and all her chatter sounded false. The hair, which was thrown crazily in all directions, in multicoloured tresses, did not help in any way to take the tension out the atmosphere.

Neither did the way she used to crease her forehead for no reason when she wanted to seem very attentive. On top of all that, I had gone there so that I could talk, not listen to her! I think I've read that was how psychotherapy is done! Well, maybe her technique was to talk ceaselessly so that she would get me talking, but it proved to be a useless technique. It all went badly, and I didn't go there any more. I then tried with a man as well – as a psychotherapist, I want to say! – but it did not work with him either. I think he would have preferred to shag me, rather than cure me. He was not lacking in charm, but that was not the reason why I went to him. He did not seem to be a Rasputin either. The good part is that I still seemed desirable to him.

Now, if Sabina gave me this notebook which is so attractive, so pleasant to touch, so beautiful, with pages that seem to be so desirous to be covered, maybe it would be good to try it in writing? Let me try, therefore. I'll see what comes out. I shall replace names of persons and localities with arbitrarily chosen letters, because I would not like to do harm to anyone, in case my notes fall into somebody's hands. It's not that my present husband – my consort, as I pet him verbally when he is not present – would be jealous, because he isn't – and this annoys me above any measure! But what if he stumbles upon the notebook by mistake? What if somebody else stumbles upon it? It is better like this, without precise references, it is better. And maybe I should dedicate these notes, this confession, these fragments from the story of my life, to Sabina, the poor darling, because she gave me the notebook. Yes, I dedicate them to her!

Events presented in leaps of time from totally different periods of my life – I cannot hold the line not even when I talk, not to mention when I write! I would like to recount them, more or less, simultaneously. That is to say, I would like to be able to write on a page the story of my teenage years. Then on the page underneath, I would cause to appear, the story of my maturity. These would be just as in my thoughts, with the first accounts superimposed by means of some kind of transparent pages, in the way photo albums of the 60s used to, those with pages made of black cardboard, each with a waxed, semi-transparent page in between made of a special paper. They have always attracted me in an inexplicable fashion. I was attracted in the same way to the pleated paper wrappings, again white and semi-transparent, in which they put chocolate bonbons, and which enchanted and took me with my thoughts to some unlived times of long ago, the time of our romantic grandmothers in long skirts falling in folds. I remember the way I looked for the boxes, which were hidden by mother in the most different places, not so that I wouldn't eat, as she didn't keep the candy for herself, but so that I wouldn't eat them all in one go.

These superimposed points of view could work out if I wrote on a website, on a blog, as one calls these thingies where everybody pours everything that passes through their minds. But I don't have the necessary skill, nor do I want to barge into the world with these swooning matters of mine. Me – I am writing here for me, so that I can find out what I'm about, what did not work to make me so discontented with my life now, because this is not just midlife crisis. That is not all it is. In any case, in our day and age, my age is the equivalent of a thirty year old woman in the times of our great-great-grandmothers.

Somewhere in between the two stories I would like the

memories, or my comments of now, to appear. It would be in this way, by preference, that a perfect story would be written - if it were possible; and I really do not think at all of connecting it to the potential act of reading, since everything would be required to be just written, and never read by anyone, not even by myself. Here are only the thoughts which ask to be liberated, spoken, and which, especially during this last period of time, block all my other actions. In the most varied of moments, and especially, but not exclusively, my moments of loneliness, I surprise myself by whispering thoughts to myself, consisting of all kinds of ideas and texts. Some of these stem from my memory, which is truly prodigious. I can never hide myself under the pretext of forgetfulness, a fact which also presents great disadvantages, especially in relationships, and provokes me almost permanently. I have tried all kinds of pretexts under which I might withdraw my words, for example, "in fact, I have nothing to say" or – why not, more refined, more profound – "I am a desert and empty" etc. These represent all kinds of fawning over myself, meant to hide my acts of cowardice, small and great. I am as full of them as a barrel under pressure.

However, I understand now that, on the margin of forty years of age, I have managed to elucidate many of the so-called mysteries which placed a mark on my childhood, adolescence, and a great part of the years of my youth. I don't know why I always felt the need to do this, but now I have had the time to remember, or, to put it better, I remembered, that I no longer have much time to hide myself while waiting for future revelations. For years on end I tried to calm down my creative restlessness and here I am, waking up now, after snoozing for such a long time, and, after, at the same time, having stopped my readings and my writing. I am amazed and very angry about all these years, although common sense tells me that, in fact, more than certainly, *this is what had to happen*. I had to see that I cannot talk seriously to anyone, that the psychiatrists are fools when they are not completely insane. I had to receive this notebook from Sabina. I am not allowed to regret and I do not regret anything from my past, not even the things through which I have not lived, although this is inexpressibly hard for the diluted German woman in me. Perhaps without this period of spiritual accumulation, if this formula does not sound too pretentious, I would not have opened my eyes enough in order to decipher the old obsessions that have haunted me for such a long time.

Around fourteen, or maybe fifteen years of age, father brought me a thick, coffee coloured book. He gave it to me and, in his tough, rough, imperative voice he said that I must read it. A reading recommendation, but made like this, in his own style. Unmistakeable. Because it came from him, and because the rebel in me was accustomed to be opposed out of instinct, I was tempted to shelve it in the library without even casting an eye over its pages, but the exciting title attracted me and made me start reading. It was *With the Gypsy Girls and other stories*[28]. It was a kind of love at first sight and the reading marked my vision about love in a crucial, definitive manner. I was very close to writing this last word with a capital letter, and it would not have been a mistake, it would have illustrated my teenage conception about the mysterious

---

28 *La ţigănci şi alte povestiri*. Fantastic-philosophical stories by Mircea Eliade (1907-1986), Romanian writer, philosopher and historian of religions. The volume mentioned further below, published in English as *Bengal Nights*, is based on his stay in India in 1930.

sentiment. The vision? The conception? I don't have words which are more suitable than these. I remember the way I read until dawn, when I dropped flat. I remember the way I purely and simply devoured the book in the next two days or so, with a constantly increasing pleasure, the way I was drunk on emotion, the way I discovered with surprise the erotic connotations of the stories, the way I was enchanted by the thread of the narratives – because, in fact, this is what my literary and, so to speak, philosophical perception was confined to during that period of time – and the way I tried to obtain another book by the same author, which was going to happen only some years afterwards, when I found an old edition of *Maitreyi*. I found it in the decrepit travel case of an aunt, a sister of my father's, together with a multitude of inter-war magazines and some other books from around the same period. She had kept it somewhere hidden during the years of the repression and she had recovered the case only recently, in a moment of fright, and brought it home.

Back then I was a rebellious lyceum-girl full of the most stupid conceits with regard to notions such as femininity, love, sexuality etc. I was beautiful and desired, I knew this from the eyes of the men on the street, not just those of the boys in the classroom. I was a nonconformist in all and sundry, a rebel and even a bit savage. I had created for myself a sort of system of values, in the main a totally erroneous one, with very few principles, but which at least still stand even today. The fashion of the times had imposed a certain social and erotic behaviour. Couples were made and unmade with the speed of light, with joy, with indifference and even with humour. It wasn't easy to get to serious relations, or to become a stable couple, not at all.

In general, everything was kept platonic, including kisses, touches and… that's kind of it. Boys bragged when they "titted" a girl. The most courageous girls did so when they felt the boys' manhood through the wall formed by skirts and trousers. Some of them even had the courage to touch the precocious protuberances with their hands. I imposed upon myself a refusal of conformity as well, and, as far as possible, a desire to shock at any price, while playing a role which I regretted profoundly later on, that of inaccessible greatness. On top of that, I was convinced that a boy – as you could not talk about mature men as yet – had to deserve the "priceless" gift of my lips, of my breasts – and this only in an exceptional case – or, at the most, he would have to earn my acceptance to be his partner in order for us to be considered a couple. The limits which, in the end, I would have accepted to achieve in a relationship, and which I did accept, were placed more or less here. Of course, I am smiling now and sometimes I pity the gaucheness of my judgment at the time. But what nobody knew was my hidden desire, almost hidden from myself as well, to be conquered, to have a kind of miracle happen to me which would make me forget what my rationality had proposed and what I had accepted with too much ease and too seriously. Maybe I was a snob, a fool, but I liked myself back then!

That was the precise period in which I read *Maitreyi*. I was shocked. An idea emerged with blinding clarity from the reading, which my mind, as it was at the time, refused to accept. This was an idea which, unfortunately, seemed to be inconceivable until very late in the years of maturity, namely that Love – look, I finally wrote it with a capital letter! – as a sentiment and with all its spiritual implications, can be the result of physical relations. That is to say that the physical love between a man and a woman can precede love as a profound and total sentiment. Such a blow on the top of my head, such disappointment, such bewilderment! I deceived myself into the most soothing explanation, namely that *such a thing cannot happen in real life*, that such a thing happens only in books, even if it starts from real events, and that literary fiction, the story, has gone to giddy heights and surpassed reality. I therefore continued my existence, with my permissive, innocent, non-obsessive and especially virginal loves, without being troubled. That's how it is!

Coming of age brought no change in my life. My father continued to beat me, more as a preventive measure than anything else. I still addressed the greeting of "*sărumîna*" – kiss your hand – to our neighbours. I was still a rebel and a refugee in reveries, long breaks for dreaming. However, during the summer holiday after the 11th grade in school[29,] a kind of miracle took place. I was allowed to go to the seaside only with my brother and his girlfriend, both of whom were students. So we went camping with the tent to Costinești, and we were going to stay there for as long as the money lasted, to live free and unworried. I was drunk with happiness, I could not believe it, I was getting away from under the guardianship of my parents or teachers. I was taking on life on my own account. God, how happy I was!

The first days were spent in the company of some friends. One of them especially, X, was very close to me. Although he was from County Olt and rash in gestures and words, so much so that you could not manage to follow him all

---

29 The Romanian school system starts with year 1 at six or seven years of age, and finishes (with the aim of continuing to study for university education) with year 12, finalised with the baccalaureate examinations.

the time, we had many things in common. We had met some years previously and had kept the relationship going, writing tens and tens of letters, talking on the phone etc. I did not feel any attraction towards him, we were just very good buddies, or at least I liked to deceive myself with this, and, also, to brag. In fact, this story which takes a look at my good male friends is something I liked to show off for a long time, until I got near to the age of forty and near to the same limits of grace. This was when I started to see in this declaration more of my powerlessness and dissatisfaction than a reason which was worth a boast. I admit I still use this "slogan" now and then even today, more in order to mask my true nature and my convictions connected to Eros, when faced with persons from outside "my world". This way, in order to escape the chore of explanations with which I can complicate things even more, and with which I risk unleashing opprobrium, stigmatising me and my family, I prefer to make categorical declarations which consecrate me unhesitatingly as a freak. An innocent, inoffensive freak, who, nevertheless, possesses an undeniable morality.

Opening these parentheses, I feel how the spirit of Scheherazade starts to possess me, which is attractive to me now, although at the time of reading the *1001 Nights*, it bothered me and interrupted my joy in the most pleasant moments. In fact, I admit that this is a flaw of my storytelling nature; sometimes I exasperate my friends with my interruptions and large parentheses, with my incursions into other stories and memories. My luck is that I have understanding friends, who are endowed with patience, tolerance and the necessary intelligence to discriminate between essential chapters and the rest, and who, showing enviable attention, manage to bring me back to the initial thread, which I often lose when left to myself.

So I spent some nights with my friends at the seaside, after which, one evening, I was left alone with my brother, who announced that I was not allowed to come inside the tent before the habitual hour, meaning three in the morning, as if I did he was going to thrash me and break my legs. I understood the rule rapidly! Unworried about spending half of my night alone, I sat in the roots of a tree near a terrace where the band Compact from Cluj played – this was before they became big stars. They interpreted pop hits, people danced, there was light there. I was smoking filter-free *Carpați*[30] cigarettes, like almost everybody else, with the exception of the folks who could afford to buy "Americans" from the sailors, and I waited for time to pass so that I could leave for "home" at the tent, to sleep. At some point, there came a group of two very beautiful girls and two men, one of whom attracted my attention by his hippy looks, with very long, gently wavy hair, a beard, a torn yellow t-shirt and jeans. The others in the group were dressed neatly, even too decently for an evening at the seaside in Costinești. He stopped, and, his elbows leaning on the railing that separated the terrace from the copse of trees, he stayed for some minutes looking fixedly at me. Feeling somehow protected by the barrier between us, I held his gaze, hanging from it and telling him in my mind: "If you only knew how sleepy I am…" I put my hand inside the chest pocket – I was wearing black cords and an authentic *military* shirt, as per the fashion of the times, which had belonged to a soldier who sold it to me after he "disappeared" it from the army

30 *Carpați* were the cheaper Romanian cigarettes, filter-less, known as coffin nails.

– and I discovered I was left without cigarettes. Seeing that the unknown man was smoking, I lifted two fingers at him, like we did in school, and I quickly received two cigarettes, thrown into the grass near me – also filter-free *Carpați*. I lit one of them, but I did not manage to say thanks because one of the girls from the table came and pulled him by the sleeve, after which they were lost in the crowd of dancers. The band started to play *I am sailing* by Rod Stewart, but I could not enjoy the music too much because some guy appeared out of the blue, holding a bottle of wine in one hand, and took me for a dance by literally pulling me up. We danced among the trees. The guy was horrible, he was staggering, but I was afraid to reject him outright. He talked incoherently and kept trying to sneak his free hand under my shirt. Look, not even the uniform could save me! Lifting my desperate gaze to the railings, I saw again the beardy man looking attentively at me. I pulled myself from the arms of the reveller and ran to him. He stretched his hand to me naturally, caught mine and took me, as if in a dream, through chairs, tables, trees, to a quiet place behind the discotheque. On the way, with the hands that were free, we each grabbed a wooden chair on which we sat. We had not said one word yet. We both lit a cigarette. We said our names: he was Hungarian, his name was Z. and he was from B. We told jokes for hours on end, and he asked me if I wanted to dance. It had seemed to him that I was longing for it when I was sitting down looking at the people around me. I calmed him down. No, I did not want to dance, and I explained to him like a nice girl, in school, that I was forbidden to return to the tent before three o'clock in morning, because my brother was making love in there, and that, if I did, he would break my legs. He listened to me with attention, with seriousness, then he took my hand again and he told me he would take care of me until the respective hour.

He was twenty-three, he was a student at Theology in C., he came from a special family, with a father who was a lawyer and had a stormy past. A car had run him over and he was left with a slight handicap of the foot, which produced a slight wavering in him, almost unnoticeable, while walking. But I was not interested in all this. The first "miracle" – with the exception of the meeting itself – happened a short time after we were acquainted. I immediately confessed to him my love for his native town, the fact that I had spent many holidays at my relatives there, and I started suddenly to tell him of an event that had happened two years previously. It was close to the New Year, I was in B at a concert of classic guitar with a French musician as soloist. Being in the middle of the period of the celebrated electricity cuts, the light went off suddenly and the hall was enveloped by pitch darkness. Z. continued excitedly: "And then some guy from the first row lit a cigarette lighter until they brought candles – that was me!". I had noticed him in the hall at the time, too. The musician offered to play pieces at the public's request, "and a girl behind me said *Bach, s'il vous plaît*"... I interrupted him, shouting, full of joy: "That was me!".

Hours flew like long clouds over plains, we walked, we told stories, we laughed and we set up a date for the morning of the next day, at nine o'clock, under "my tree". He walked me to the tent and, when I raised my head, I met his soft, hot and dry lips – he had a strong mouth, with thick lips, firm and delicate in the same time, unforgettable. It was a heart-rending kiss and, I don't know why, after we parted I burst into tears. In the end, I was only a tired and scared child, disoriented and on the road to falling madly in love for the first time, with her destined one. But I did not know those things as yet, I could not know them. Starting from the next morning, we did not separate until the end of our holiday. We slept together, we ate, we lounged in the sun, we swam, we laughed and we cried, we recounted our past and confessed our dreams, hopes and aspirations. I was a bit frightened by his age, his erudition and life experience. He was strong and decided, but, at the same time, very affectionate and delicate. He cared for me like for a child, but he respected my needs, my wishes or simple whims. When I chased him away from me, crying, he knew to wait for me to receive him back again, which only made me regret my childish behaviour, respect and love him more. I needed him to find out who I was. And the first stage of self-knowledge took place sooner than I expected. Even from the first days he used to spoil me by massaging me all over my body. He stretched me out on a mattress and massaged me from the toes to the temples. In the beginning, everything took place in the light of day, outside, in the yard, near the tent. Nice and spoiled, semi-undressed, in a bathing suit, I unconsciously received his beneficial caresses. We then went inside the tent, where the same ritual took place, accompanied by increasingly fiery kisses all over my body. I assisted passively, and somehow inquisitively, everything that happened to me, without feeling anything special, without feeling shivers of desire. I abandoned myself exclusively to innocent pleasure and total relaxation. Then, one evening, because it was raining, I decided to break the custom of three o'clock in the morning and decided to sleep in his tent.

He camped in a yard that was on the edge of Costineşti. His tent was yellow, discoloured and patched, the zipper at the entrance was broken. Inside, a simple rucksack and a wonderful sleeping bag, thick and filled with special down, in which you could sleep even on the mountain, outside. It had a special shape, oval, somehow anatomical. I had not seen anything like that. A single person could sleep in it. He laid me down in it, it was very warm; he undressed me with care, slowly-slowly, and he stretched on the floor near me, on the naked earth, dressed. I was sleepy and I was numb, he talked slowly, very slowly, then all that was left were the kisses and his hands caressing my body, the ritual massage.

For the first time I was alone, naked, in the arms of a man and, even with all that, I was very calm and I felt safe. I had told him very proudly, from the beginning, that I was a virgin and that I intended to stay like that until my meeting with my "destined one", and he had promised he would always obey my wishes. He caressed me with indescribable gentleness, he searched every centimetre of my body. His hand went lower for the first time to my sex, which was released from the protection of the slip. He covered it with his hand, he caressed me gently and, just as gently, almost unperceivable, his finger started to penetrate me, to caress my clitoris, of which I became conscious for the first time. I felt my heartbeat descending in my sex and booming simultaneously somewhere in my brain. Something was ready to escape out from me. I felt a warm moisture surging from me, I started to move instinctively. I felt my vagina rebelling, and thirsty with the wait, I wanted him to penetrate me deeper, but he always returned, careful, to a safer area. I was ashamed, but I could not stop. Time disappeared and I thought that was everything there was to it, that anything more was not possible, that I had reached the apogee, when orgasm took me by surprise, making me tense my entire body and moan with pleasure and joy, and all the accumulated rebelliousness of the vagina dissipated into a kind warmth. I barely had the strength to ask what had happened to me and *if I was a virgin still.* He laughed quietly, kissed me, held me in his arms next to him, but I was impatient to find out what had happened, and I suddenly became aware of everything that surrounded me, of the tent's door that was moving, of the rain that was falling, of his hard sex adhering to my hip, and not for one moment did I think of him, I savoured all my sensations alone, I lived the joy of discovering my own body, without being aware of the presence of the man near me. I fell asleep smiling in his arms, knowing that something had changed forever.

Starting from the next morning, I found myself looking at him with different eyes. I would study his traits with attention, his arms, his muscles, and for the first time I lowered my eyes to the protuberance of his sex through the underpants. I started to caress him in my turn, to kiss him at my own initiative. I petted him, I clung to his body in every way. I stroked my breasts all over his body and I invented the most wonderful positions and touches. I used each time that we bathed in the sea for new erotic games. I sneaked under the water and bit his arms, his legs, his loins, his neck, his cheeks. I discovered an animal in me who was willing to offer and receive pleasure in any place, under any guise. Back then I did not know that such behaviour could drive a man mad. I did not know I was producing pleasures but also pains which were equally great. I was all instinct

81

and too little conscience. I was woman in woman's pure state, unadulterated by education, formalism or vices. After that night he did not touch me again, the miracle was not repeated. I now know that he would have been able to stop, once my unchained femininity had demanded its rights.

I shall now have to add an essential comment. No one, not even one of the men that followed – not that there were very many of them – has managed to awaken in me that pure, devastating instinct. I always hoped and dreamed of the magic of that first night. I compared all my erotic experiences with what had happened back then, but I never again vibrated with desire as in that night. It was not fated to me to, I did not know how to choose the appropriate man, I did not know how I should be, what to do, I don't know where the truth is. I only know that tens of years afterwards I lived without love, that my friends, readings, and quotidian adventures were the pitiful substitute of the love I was not fated to have ever again. Not one God-given day passed without me thinking of the mistake I made, even the sacrilege I committed in refusing love – the one with capital *L*, goddammit! – when it had been offered to me. The events that followed proved to me that he was the "chosen one", and I did not know it, did not see it, I had been blind, very young and damned stupid. I did not know what I should have done and now I sit here, hidden in the kitchen, and torment this notebook.

Returning to our story, we prolonged our sojourn at the seaside as much as we could. On returning, we passed through B., and I met a part of his family there, I visited his house. I thought I loved him, when in fact I loved the man from my magic night, the other one – the real one, so to speak – who inspired, instead, admiration, respect, and somehow fear with regard to a future which was much too certain and too serious when compared to the irresponsible way I was accustomed to live. He presented to me a future which was much too normal, concretised in marriage, family, children etc. I did not really see myself in such a position, me as a student at some Polytechnic and him a Reform priest! In the following period we wrote tens of letters – I keep all his letters even today, after almost twenty-five years, the most wonderful love letters anyone ever wrote to me. I felt venerated like a princess, and I was just a child, a woman in the making. We even managed to meet again in C. for some minutes, afterwards. I was in year 12. I was at the school one day and during one of the breaks a colleague announced me that a "gentleman" was looking for me. My legs were cut from under me when I saw him. It was him indeed, my lover, but without jeans, without a beard and rebellious locks, dressed correctly in clothes cut from fabric and a trench coat of ash-coloured balloon cloth. He smelled of tobacco and "old" man – he was almost twenty-four years of age! – we walked and I felt embarrassed by his "normal", banal, classic and much, much too nice aspect. I was spiteful because he had nothing left of the rebellious air of last summer. I was scared by his seriousness, I was frightened by the solemnity in his voice, I was inhibited and I think I behaved stupidly. Yes, he was, as my schoolmate had said, "a gentleman". After his departure, I made my letters scarcer, I no longer replied and, slowly-slowly, everything was extinguished. I would think of him many times, especially at night, when I seemed to hear his voice calling me, and I would wake up scared, seeming to feel him near me. Some years passed by. During the university, I got married to a colleague with whom we had a wonderful communication on the intellectual side… and that was kind of it. He was not my "chosen one", not even by a distance. He was somehow my father's involuntary chosen one! Again from a spirit of rebelliousness, in order to confront my father and to escape his preventive beatings, I married the first man to whom I could talk.

I no longer knew anything about Z, for some good years, when, one summer night, being in the house of my husband – my first husband – in the town of A., I woke up scared, "hearing" again the voice of Z. calling me and asking me what he should do. The impression was so strong, so shocking, especially because I wouldn't hear voices all day long, that I did not manage to fall back asleep again. I waited for the appropriate hour and called him. I had kept his home number from B. I think it was on a Sunday. His mother answered, and, after I asked for him on the phone, she replied in extremely correct sentences: "No, Maria, it is already late for you. Z. is no longer home, he is having his wedding today". I hung up the phone. It was then that I cried for the first time for him, after him, feeling that I had lost him forever.

After more than ten years, this strange longing caught me again, madly. I looked him up with a great effort and I managed to trace him again. Even more, I talked to him on the phone, and emotions altered my voice, but even so he recognised me immediately, although it had been almost fifteen years since the last time we had talked. I asked him if he could forgive me, and he said something amazing: "Of course, Maria, love of my life. What forgiveness can you be talking about?".

I started to cry again, I asked him a great deal of stupid

things, about his family, his job, his mother, etc. and I noticed with surprise that he knew a great many things about me. I did not have the courage to propose a meeting, although I wanted it, I wanted it madly. I was content with his laughter and forgiveness. I sent him a huge envelope containing a photograph of mine, a letter in which I confessed my love in a veiled manner, as well as photocopies of all the letters I had received from him. I don't know why I did that. I don't know if he ever got the envelope. What is certain is that, for a while, I found my peace again.

After some other years, a witch, an old Hungarian Gypsy who knew absolutely nothing about me, said this: "The only one that would have mattered was the Hungarian, but you wanted to miss that train." I was left perplexed by her words. I knew for certain that the happiness he could have given me was not happiness I got from any of the men in my life – who haven't been many, as I said before – because I always longed and looked for the perfect sentiment, complete and round, with which I had woken up in his arms in my first morning as a woman. Although I would think of him very often, I no longer had the courage to look him up, until this spring, when I dared again. I talked with him, he was warm, good and affectionate, but I realised I no longer have a place in his life, that he is a man who is much too busy, with an important position within his church and too little spare time at his disposal. I felt stupid for my insistence; but now, now that we have started to talk again, the modern means of communication, the mobile phone, email, text message, make our closeness easier. I had started to dream of a possible meeting in October, when I was going to pass through B. I looked him up on the phone yesterday, but he was in a meeting. I decided to stop any attempt to contact him until he should show the wish to have me one way or another in his life, but last night I received a text message from him in which he wrote: "Life is beautiful, it's just that it runs past us, and we pant following it, and then we wake up to find we were left on the outside. Only meetings? Only work? I call you today!"

I wait for the follow-up with all my soul, the rounding off of the story under one shape or another, the end. Yes, I am not only a silly romantic, but also a Bovary-like over-romantic, straightforwardly stupid! Tens of years on the tracks of a chimera... But what if, what if...

(Here end the jottings in the notebook.)

November 2010

The Unhappy Adventure of My Friend Adam Leon – a Professor, a Literary Man, a Photographer and a Martyr

A Worthy Pillar of Letters, an Arbiter of Elegance...

My friend Adam Leon is one of the best known literary men in our conurbation and probably, despite his rather sporty attire, a kind of arbiter of masculine elegance. He is pretty tall, supple, like a man who moves around more than between the bed and his car, and more than between the car and his place of destination. He is always dressed comfortably, but everything also matches – if he wears a jacket, everything will of course be aligned to that, from the top of his socks to that of the tie– and always in clothes of very good quality. If he's wearing jeans, he doesn't get lower than Levi Strauss. His pullovers are one hundred percent wool, preferably Shetland, his shirts are English, his shoes are stitched by hand, his t-shirts are from Gucci or Dior, his socks are always of cotton and his ties always of the finest silk. At the age of slightly over fifty years at the moment of this unprecedented event, he was a rather pleasant presence, not only because of his young face, because of the mane which he allowed to flow down his back, and because of the brown, lively, scrutinising eyes, which were, nevertheless, somehow melancholy and warm; but also because of an amiability which was equal to itself, worthy of being shared with any interlocutor, with everybody. Maybe it was also a kind of self-protective shield, but it was also a very efficient mechanism in his relations with the people around.

This amiability of course required effort and partitioned his time energetically. He could not refuse an invitation to a book launch, to a televised show, and not even one to some baptism, wedding or funeral, although events of this kind were not precisely his greatest weakness. Sure, he liked to be present in the public life of the city, but he would have liked to be able to select his occasions on a more personal and parsimonious basis. He knew too well that an excessive presence ends up eroding a public image, but God or nature, despite the numerous gifts with which they had endowed him, had not offered him the one gift of the power to refuse. So it was that he used to spend a good part of his spare time – if he still had anything like it – replying to diverse requests and regretting almost every time this cursed inability to refuse. However, this does not mean that he squandered all his time exactly. Besides the classes at the University, where he was brilliant in his literature courses, and despite the numerous cultural-society obligations which I had just evoked, he was able to find time to write and publish in the cultural press, with a certain regularity, cultivated and erudite essays on literature, which he collected periodically in volumes which were well received by the connoisseurs and his colleagues, the literary critics. He even published, from time to time, volumes of poems which were of a perhaps exacerbated sensitivity, but also of an irreproachable stylistic refinement. All this on the background of a certain melancholy, which was more of a culturally acquired habit that had settled in his essence by the means of reading, rather than a structural melancholy.

Anyway, news about his knowledge, and that he was an excellent specialist, had travelled. His reputation was not only because of his solid philological education, collected from other people's books, as one might say, but also from his own constant experience of writing. So that, because of his inability to refuse, he was always besieged by the colleagues who wanted to find out his opinion on some manuscript, by young beginners who submitted to his attention their debut volumes in almost all literary genres, by non-literary folks who believed their life was a novel and wanted to prove this in writing as well, by others who believed they could not leave the world widowed of their memoirs or childhood recollections. Almost everywhere in the house, mixed through real books in the course of being read, between literary magazines or those from the field of philology, you could chance upon print-outs of the most varied literary or para-literary manuscripts, upon debut volumes or notebooks written by skilled or less skilled hands.

Other such attempts lurked on the screen of the monitor, not getting to be printed out as yet, or not being ready to be on paper at all, making even more demands from eyes which had already lingered too long in front of the luminescent screen. This is what he was like, however, this is how he is, the amiable Adam Leon, the man who is incapable of refusing anybody. Truth is that the petitioners did not besiege him entirely for nothing. He always read attentively the things that were offered to him, he proposed solutions which the authors had not thought about, he even corrected the style if the case called for it, and he did not refuse to write a preface if he was asked to do so. Even more, his amiability had no limits if he chanced upon a manuscript which was truly very good. He could talk about anything and everything forever with the editors of magazines or publishing houses he knew, in order to promote that particular literary product; and he was often successful, because his taste was unquestionable – a collection of poetry in a magazine, a fragment of prose or an essay in another, an article of support in some other one. In happy hours, he even succeeded in promoting the publication of the manuscript in full by a publishing house disposed to assume the financial risks of the adventure. In his own way, he was a strange phenomenon in the republic of the letters, which is governed rather by envy and jealousy than by excesses of generosity. However, this is what he was like. When he read a manuscript or book, he was actually glad, although he was not the author, but sometimes he was the midwife, and at other times the godfather.

Of course, generosity, the incapacity to refuse, and literary curiosity also played tricks on him on a few occasions. It happened at times that some student or PhD candidate would look for a less known foreign author, to translate them into Romanian and to propose the text for a reading. This was not out of a desire for literary glory, nor purely and simply in order to trick him. It was done searching for a bridge which would allow access to a different intimacy than that connected to literature as such. The vanity of his correspondents was also a problem. One of his inflexible principles was "never with students". A sort of kleptomaniac and mythomaniac had tried to trick him once. He had approached with a whole dossier of stolen works, all passed through a kind of personal filter, beyond the variety of the stolen authors' style, as if he had not managed to succeed fully in the process of identifying himself with any of them. Adam Leon's pretty rich and varied reading generally helped him to manage things in such circumstances, but he also had a kind of sixth sense, which was rather well developed and trained. All this showed him people's intention as a kind of filigree image; but he had been very near to sending such fakery to the printers a few times. Praise the Heavens, something had stopped him in the last moment. Well, it was this somewhat paternal generosity again – we have to mention here that he had no children, although he had been married for a while – that led him into the entanglement he recounted to me over a glass of old whisky and an aromatic coffee in the work studio of his home.

An invasion at dawn...

"As I was saying, I was home alone for some days, Marta being away at her excavations looking for vestiges of the past. I had stayed awake a little later in the evening, so that I could read a bit more from a book I was going to introduce at a launch event and, if it convinced me enough, also to write an article about it. I had set the phone to wake me up at eight in the morning so that I could continue my read and possibly jot down some things, because around lunchtime I still had some running to do, and the event was fixed for five in the afternoon. I was not necessarily under pressure, but circumstances called for me to work pretty tightly, so that I would have my homework ready at the appropriate moment."

He stopped a little, as if searching for words, he – a spontaneous and fluent speaker, precisely those qualities which contributed to the charm of his classes, of the conferences or of the speeches at various cultural and social events. He started to talk again. He was telling the story with some difficulty, with pauses and repetitions, and with clarifications after other stretches of the story, so I shall try to make a summary, as far as possible, of his incredible adventure on a beautiful morning at the end of one spring. Events which in life are disjointed, lacunar, repetitive, stammered, cannot stay the same in literature because you risk being accused of a lack of coherence by the critics. Although, in the end, we are not talking about literature here, but about the attempt to help a friend who had experienced severe trials. As Adam went on with the story, I could hear his wife in the other rooms, making normal, calm movements. She did not make any demonstrative noises, it did not even seem to me that she was trying to eavesdrop.

So, Adam had gone to bed rather late and had set the telephone to wake him up at eight. While he was asleep, the phone started to ring. He heard the ringing, at first in his sleep, then also a noise, a sort of rumbling coming from the small table at the bedhead. To make more certain that he would hear it, he had set it to vibrate, and had set the alarm on "repeat". In the end, still half asleep, eyes closed, he stretched out his hand to the apparatus and placed it next to his ear, at the same time pushing the button to take the call, understanding that it was not the alarm ringing his wakeup call. He mumbled a "hello", while opening his eyes with difficulty, casting a look at the wall clock. It was not even six! He almost let go a curse, stopping it at the back of his throat with difficulty, not without regrets, but his good breeding probably did not desert him even in his sleep. The voice from the receiver said: "it's Lia, I've just reached the train station. Are you coming to see me? Sorry for this too early morning hour, but the train has just arrived. It was more than ten hours from Cluj to your town. The station building is beautiful. I had a coffee here, but I don't like the area, only the station". The female voice rattled on at speed, offering a lot of information which he did not need; not at this hour, anyway, and suddenly awoken from his sleep. He did not like to wake up like that, he preferred to stretch like a cat for a minute or two before standing up. For the first moment, he understood practically nothing. Lia who? What train station? What business did he have with one or the other? He would have slept for another two hours without this imbecile phone call, and then he would have woken up slowly, just the way he liked it. Under the impact of the shock, he started to wake up anyway, and replied that it was a matter of a quarter of an hour to get there. She should look around the train station some more until he did so. While saying these words to her, he looked around the room for some clothes in which to get dressed immediately. He saw them, but he could have taken a longer time, so that he would get to drink at least the first of his morning coffees, without which he was not functional. And yet…

He dressed automatically, as fast as he could, regretting at the same time that he was giving an approval to the request, and thoughts started to arrange themselves in some sort of order. Yes, Lia, that girl from *Ardeal* who works in Strasbourg, an interpreter, a translator, something of this kind, for those European institutions which nobody keeps count of anymore. He had read some manuscripts, he had edited them a little, too. She was talented, in more directions as well; he had read a volume of poetry, one of short prose and two small novels. Well written, with imagination. He had also put together two prefaces for her, one for the volume of poems and the other for one of the micro-novels, the one that had appeared afterwards in French at what was probably a very small publishing house he had not heard of. He had been in correspondence with her in the period when he was reading her attempts, he had even connected her to the publishing houses here, not the big ones, some smaller ones, but demanding enough in their selections, even if they normally published at the authors' expense, through the sponsorships they had attracted, or by making appeals to all kinds of local or central funding for "the support of written culture". Beyond these financial issues, the problem with these small publishing houses was also, that because they did not have large scale distribution services, the road to their readership was totally random. Yes, he remembered that he had put together for Lia a long list of literary personalities her books should have reached, and to whom she should send books in the mail, if she also wanted to have readers who were qualified up to some point. He had seen some articles about her in the cultural press, he had noticed her name in diverse evaluations in the balance sheet articles, which meant she had followed his advice, that is, if it was not the case that she had perhaps paid for them, because she seemed to be trained in slightly more capitalistic cultural mechanisms. She had sent him via Western Union several hundreds of Euros for his efforts of reading and editing, although he had not asked for anything of the sort. He had tried to mount a kind of timid protest, but in the end he had accepted the money, of course, not just because an extra coin doesn't harm anyone, but also because Lia was not inclined to have a discussion about this aspect.

Well, this was Lia, he had found her, but what had come over her with this unannounced trip? What the devil did she want from him at six o'clock in the morning? He was already en route to the train station, he lived close enough, in the centre of town, and the train station, which had been probably located closer to the edge of the place when it had been built, had somehow reached the central area as well. There was no use climbing behind the wheel. He would not have had good enough reflexes. It would not have made sense to grab a taxi either; he was too near, and furthermore he was also becoming more awake by walking in a pretty alert rhythm, given the context of waking up – or that of still being asleep.

She was where he had told her to wait, near a kiosk with a railing used to rest coffee glasses on, and she was just sipping from one. He recognised her immediately, although he had only seen her in the photographs on the published books which she had sent him each time, including the little novel translated into French. She was smaller in height than he had imagined considering the long shape of her cheeks. She was mignon, as it were, and, to stay in the francophone area, she was a kind of *fausse maigre*, a false skinny woman. She was thin, but she had curves, as could be seen because of the figure-hugging jeans and t-shirt. The problem was whether her name really was Lia, because she used more than one e-mail address, under different names. She had signed the volumes from Romania with one of them, but the one from France under a French pseudonym. He could not understand why she proceeded in this manner. Maybe the young woman felt she had a type of multiple personality, maybe she wanted to hide behind these multiple identities. In any case, what did it matter? He was there, in the train station, some twenty metres away from her, woken up with the night still in his head and with the clearly emerging thought that he had to drink a coffee urgently, before anything else. It was not quite before anything else, because she had also perceived him very quickly, come some metres forward to welcome him, perched on her toes, embraced him a little too warmly for the degree of their acquaintance, and even tried to kiss him on the mouth. He barely managed to turn his face a little and to receive the kiss on his cheek. He answered with a rather more conventional kiss on the cheek and, giving as a reason that he urgently needed a coffee, he moved towards the kiosk in front of which were her bags and the coffee she had already begun. He asked what she was doing there and why she had not, at least, given him a sign beforehand. In the meantime, he got his coffee, with milk and too sweet, because the seller poured sugar out of a jar with a metal spout, instead of offering sachets of sugar so that you can use as much as needed, and, while labouring with the eccentric product, he also received his answers. She had come to the home country to see her family, and she had come here to thank him directly and personally for the support he had provided for her literary beginnings. She also had some gifts for him, which she could not have sent in the post as they were unspeakably fragile, and, since she was there, she also wanted to see the town, which she had seen only once before, on the run, when she was a lyceum student and had taken part in I don't know what Olympic exams, probably of the literature kind.

They could see on the train station's clocks that it was close to seven. He proposed to lead her to a hotel, in the centre of the town, some hundreds of metres away, and then, after she changed clothes, going out somewhere in order to have breakfast. She replied, smiling, that they rent the rooms at lunchtime in hotels, and it would be better for them to go to his house first, refresh herself, catch her breath, and drink a proper coffee together, then go out in the town afterwards. That didn't sound good to him. Furthermore, as he had been alone for more than one week, the house was not too tidy, and, what's more, he was somehow reluctant about people inviting themselves. On the other hand, even if this was involuntary, he was still some kind of a host and a guide. So it is that, without finishing the ill-fated coffee, he shouldered the rather big, but otherwise not very heavy travel bag, and they left together towards the town centre, without getting a taxi. He lived too near for that, as I already said.

"Old man, we were home in a matter of minutes. I unlocked the gate mechanically, then the door. I asked her in, entered after her, closed the door, and went to my workroom in front of her, asking myself in my thoughts how widespread the disorder was inside. It was widespread enough! So, after I turned on the coffee-maker, which I had managed to fill-up before going to the train station, I picked up some of the clothes that were scattered everywhere, stacked some books, arranged some papers and, as she was still standing, I invited her to take a seat in a newly-freed armchair. I asked her whether she wanted to take a bite of something and she replied that she would like to drink something with the coffee, two or three finger-widths of scotch, if I had any. I didn't have scotch, but I had some Irish whiskey, I think it was Bushmills. It was rather too early in the morning for me, but I poured some into two glasses, with maybe a little less in mine. Then I poured the hot coffee into two cups and also, sat in an armchair. We clinked glasses, after which she started to talk about all and sundry to be found under the moon and the stars, jumping from one subject to another, according to a logic which I could not manage to grasp – from visiting her parents to her architect husband, and from what else she wrote to questions about what I was writing now.

She spoke not only in a loose, disconnected way, but also somehow precipitately, during which time she finished her glass and poured herself a new one. Just as suddenly, she stopped talking, stood up from the armchair and started to go round the room, looking at the books in my library. In that moment I asked myself whether she behaved like this because she was in a new environment, in the presence of a person whom she had never seen *face to face*, whether it was the effect of tiredness accumulated on the road, coupled with the whiskey she had drunk rather too quickly, or whether she was perhaps not completely sound in her mind. In yet another sudden movement she sat down in the armchair and told me yes, she would take a bite of something now. There was not much in the refrigerator, but I managed to cobble together on a platter some *caşcaval* cheese, ham, olives and some pieces of smoked fish, shark, salmon – well, things which go well with a glass of the strong stuff. I also found a piece of rather stale bread, as I had not bought any for some two days. I asked her whether I should go out and buy fresh bread, as the store was near, but she said there was no need, that she didn't eat much bread anyway, and that she didn't want to deprive herself of my presence, not for one second. This made me fall to thinking again, but I tried to take it as some kind of joke."

They picked at something or other, drank another mouthful of whiskey, and it seemed she had become calmer. He refilled the cups of coffee and peace descended, but it did not last long. The woman stood up suddenly, went out to the hallway and returned with the other travel bag, the smaller one which he had believed to be lighter, but wasn't. "Here is your gift, look in the bag, which you can also keep." Opening the bag, he started to take out: a small wooden crate with two bottles of 18-year old Glenfiddich, a Kenzo little case with perfume, deodorant and shower gel, a few boxes of Muratti Ambassador cigarettes, and, on top of that, wrapped, an Italian shirt complete with its silk tie.

"How the devil did she know about all that, old man? I do not think that in our messages, which were exclusively literary, we had ever talked about my tastes! Do you realise that? I had not smoked Muratti for quite a while, and from my photos published in magazines she could not know what kind of shirts and ties I preferred. In the morning, before leaving, I remember precisely that I hesitated between using Davidoff or Kenzo! In the end, I used Kenzo, identical to the one which she had brought! By all the devils, I could not understand one thing. Before opening the bag, I was thinking to refuse the gifts, but on seeing them, I realised I would keep them!".

While taking the gifts from the bag, he had analysed them and, frankly, he had rejoiced in them. She was sitting quietly in the armchair, smiling playfully, and somehow in a complicit manner. He thanked her and started to arrange the gifts in places which were more suitable than the little table near the two armchairs. The shirt and tie in a drawer, the boxes of Muratti in another one, after he had taken two packs out and placed them on the table. He asked her if she didn't want to change drinks, whether they should open one of the bottles she had brought, but she replied dryly and somehow languidly, lengthening the vowels a little: "Everything is for you". She then asked for permission to go to the bathroom, to take a shower and change her clothes. Of course, like any civilised man who is kind to his guests, even though they may be uninvited, he answered in the affirmative. She took the bigger bag with her and entered the bathroom. He lit the first Muratti after a good many years in which he could not find such a thing either in Romania, or on his trips abroad. He liked the smoke, dragging it deeply in his lungs, thinking to himself that this Mary Christmas who had arrived in deep summer was rather odd, but that maybe she was not actually as mad as it had initially seemed to him, because of the agitation which appeared to haunt her. He felt good sunk in the armchair, the cigarette in one hand and the glass in the other. He was thinking of taking Lia out in town after she came out of the bathroom, and escorting her to a fancy and pretentious restaurant, so he waited for her to come out, although it seemed to him that she was staying for rather too long in there.

"Well, old man, she came out of the bathroom, and she had changed too. She was barefoot, her hair was wet, and she was wearing Marta's bathrobe! This last displeased me profoundly, because you know how careful Marta is with her personal items. She also smelled of Marta's bath salts and mousses. I was already a little scared. What if she was mad, after all? Or, even worse, a nymphomaniac? She came quickly and plumped herself in the armchair, sitting somehow in a ball, as if she were cold. Even if everything was for me, as she had said, she took a Muratti from the pack I had opened, although she still had Marlboros in her own pack, lit it with my lighter, although hers was, I believe, closer, and she then took the coffee cup I had just refilled. After a few puffs on the cigarette, she put it in the ashtray and took the cup in both her hands, as if she wanted to warm herself up. She was unexpectedly silent, almost absent. This did not last long. After some minutes, she placed the cup on the table, and started to look me fixedly in the eye, which I did too, so that I was taken completely by surprise when I felt her toes caressing me gently on the leg and advancing dangerously towards a more intimate area. I felt a sort of short-circuit through my whole body. But not because of the pleasure; anyway, not just the pleasure, but rather because of a fright. I withdrew further into the armchair, scared, sticking my legs together energetically. It might be pleasant, it might be sexy to be picked up by a woman, but it was not my style, or at least not this aggressively. Probably because I had been raped by the nanny when I was five and by another woman when I had just turned twelve! I think I told you about this before. She started to laugh quietly and, in her opinion, seductively. But I was the last human in the world who could have been seduced at that time! I had the sensation that I was going to be left forever with a castration complex. She said that she could not understand why I did not want to accept her way of thanking me. I replied that, if I wanted and agreed to be thanked in this manner every time I supported a girl in her literary beginnings, I would have probably been ground into bone china pots and mugs due to exhaustion. If I accepted this from the boys too, as we have now joined Europe, I would have been worn out even in half the time. I don't think she heard me. She repeated obsessively that she had to thank me, that she was no whore, that she didn't do this with just anyone, but that I was a special person, from whom she had received the greatest help in this unfortunate life, help which had not come from any other place. After this, seemingly forgetting what she had just said to me, she recited a long list of personalities with whom she had gone all the way, Romanian and foreign names, among whom there were Houellebecq and Bergenbier, sorry, that's the beer, so Houellebecq and Weyergans. She was, practically, delirious. It was clear, she was mad. But it was not only that. In the most dialectically possible manner, she was also clearly a nymphomaniac. How the devil could I calm her down? It's good I was living in a house instead of I don't know on what floor in a block, so the madwoman could not jump from the window! Should I give her a tranquiliser? After this much whiskey?!"

Adam was reliving the scene from some five years ago. He was agitated when he recounted the story and, despite the temporal distance and the forced humour, he seemed to be revisiting the emotions from back then. This discussion was pretty amusing. I had to make an effort in order to suppress the laughter that was ready to invade me from time to time. I had probably not managed to suppress my smile, since he said to me: "Laugh if you want to, this is certainly something to laugh at as well, even if I don't feel like laughing myself!".

I did not laugh. I respected his discomfort in the end, because I felt he had not asked me there for nothing. He was not telling the story for the sake of the story, which, and I felt this as well, had not finished at that time, a whole five-year plan period of time ago. Furthermore, I was interested in the whole story, in its ending or endings. So, I calmed him down amicably and asked him to tell me more. In some way or other, he had also managed to calm Lia *Ciocîrlia* down, as he said he had called her as a joke – she, the one who, instead of a skylark had proved to be more of a staunch, merciless woodpecker[31]! He had calmed her, but not completely, not finally. She said to him that, if he did not feel like making love, for the moment, as she hurried to add, he should at least take some nude pictures of her. He agreed, what else could he do? At least, for the time being, he had escaped the torment! He remembered clearly how she untied the cord of the bathrobe herself, how she started to pose lasciviously, wrapping the bathrobe around her, then opening its skirts or taking it off completely. At one moment, she lounged, took a banana from the platter and started to caress herself with it on the lower part of the abdomen, on the inner side of her thighs, and even higher. She would say something obscene from time to time, like a porn film actress who had inhabited her role completely. He took about fifteen pictures, all of them headless, as she had told him to leave the face outside of the frame. He took the pictures as if on autopilot, almost without looking, without joy, without feeling, like a robot. When she'd had

---

31 *Ciocîrlie* is a skylark, and the name Lia rhymes naturally with this noun. Also, *Lia Ciocîrlia* is a fairytale character. *Woodpecker* is a derogatory term for a nagging woman, as it is said to knock (metaphorically speaking) on people's head incessantly, just like the woodpecker knocks on trees.

enough of being photographed, probably also because she had not obtained the effect she had hoped for, she wrapped the bathrobe to her throat, took the Bushmills bottle, filled both glasses almost to the top and asked him: "Well, what are we going to do now?".

He hurried to propose a sortie into the town to show it to her, and possibly to take lunch. She agreed – adding, again with a smile on her lips, that she wanted to have some *stiff* red wine with the meal and that she would show him the *ins and outs* of it when they returned home again. As the danger seemed to veer away he also smiled, to some extent ironically, to some extent idiotically, pretending that he had to water some plants in the garden while she got dressed.

While he watered the plants, he saw her come out of the house dressed in different clothes, hands in pockets and a cigarette in the corner of her mouth. He convinced her that she also had to take her bags in order to make a booking in the hotel, assuring her that, after the meal, they would return to his house. They left for the town. On the road, he asked himself whether he should make a break "before or after the meal", that is, whether they would eat together. It would have been polite to take lunch, but his fear was greater than his politeness. He booked a room for her in the hotel, leaving her to take up the luggage by herself, and, when he was certain she was already up there, he left the hotel and broke into a run, rounding the corner of a block of flats nearby. As he suspected she remembered the way, he didn't even go home, but to some relatives, waiting for the book launch there and perpetually looking at the door in fear, asking himself whether he had told her anything about the event and whether the organisers had displayed posters. He was hoping they had not! Despite the fact that he had not managed to finish reading the book, and that he did not have his notes on him, his performance was brilliant, maybe even above average in respect to his usual performances.

After the usual glass of champagne at the end, he started for his home, looking around him with extreme attention, even increasing his concentration when closer to the house, if such a thing were possible. It seemed that everything was in order, so he leapt at the door and entered the house just as quickly, drew all curtains that were not yet drawn, turned on a light in the hallway, which was not visible from the outside, and switched on a small lamp on the desk in his workroom. He sat in the armchair, inhaled deeply, lit a Muratti from the pack forgotten on the table when they had gone out, poured the last finger of drink from the bottle on the table and, opening a bottle of still water, he told himself that he was now starting to calm down. He was thinking that, in the end, it was good he didn't have a heart condition, because he could not say how he might have escaped from this story if that was the case. In the end, he stood up and, going to the desk, he turned on the computer, transferred the photographs from the camera to a folder baptised ad-hoc as "Capture", then opened the e-mail and sent the photographs in a few successive messages to one of her e-mail addresses. He immediately erased the photos from the camera, but, as it will be seen afterwards, not those he had transferred to the computer.

Epilogue after Five Years...

"Well, old man, up to this point, everything is simple and even worthy of being laughed at if it does not concern you directly, and I would not have been upset by it if you had laughed. But it is only now, after almost five years, that the truly sinister part begins. It is precisely because of this that I asked you to come and that I recounted all this matter which is somewhat surreal, if not extra-terrestrial. You know I've been to Bucharest, at Bookfest. I was invited by some authors and editors to talk at some launches. I do not like launches at fairs because everything is noisy, people circulate all over the place, they pass through the launch space as well, and you can't understand one thing about it all. However, I went there because it is one of the few occasions when I can see acquaintances from all over the country, not just Bucharest natives, and, on top of that, I can also find a book which has either escaped my notice or which I hadn't heard of at the moment of its launch. Well. Saturday morning, on the day I left for home, I woke up earlier in order to make a last visit, but I got there before closing time, so I entered the Press Centre in order to check my electronic correspondence. When I entered my address, surprise: three messages from Marta, all with attachments. But the joy was of a short duration – even in the small format of the attachments I recognised a part of the photos I had taken five years ago. Of the messages themselves I won't say anything more: shameless, divorce, my bathrobe, our house, and all and sundry that can be imagined in such situations. What the devil could I say to her? I replied at first that I did not understand a thing, because I actually did not, I had completely forgotten that I hadn't deleted the pictures from the computer as well. I was thinking this is an entrapment etc. Then I picked up on the fact that in the third message there was a nude photo dated this year, which was certainly not taken by me. It was a photograph I had received, and it had seemed to me to be artistically made, which was why I had kept it somewhere on the computer, maybe even on the desktop. Marta was connected, she replied immediately that the other photos were, in fact, taken by me, which I had no way of denying.

We exchanged some more messages. She seemed increasingly neurotic, me – increasingly scared; and before leaving the computer I wrote a message with the already classic reply: this is not what you think, nor is it what you see. This is indeed all that it was. For some days now, since I came back, I moved into this room. She does not even reply when I greet her. I don't know what to say to her, how to explain. If I tell her exactly how things happened, I have no chance of being believed. Who would believe such aberration? I was thinking you might help me. That you might write this story and then publish it as soon as possible. On the blog, because it works the fastest and you've published literature on it before. Maybe this way she will understand it. This is what I want from you, old man. Why am I not writing it? I would not be credible and I have never written fiction either!"

Of course I had and still have my doubts with regard to literature's power to influence reality in such a radical manner, but what could I do? I promised I was going to write the story which, look – is just ending, and that I would publish it on the blog, which I shall do immediately after I have re-read it and made the necessary corrections. As for the effect hoped for by my friend Adam, I continue to have great doubts, but who knows? I do believe him, something as hallucinating as this is hard to imagine, and on top of that I also studied his face while he was speaking, but it does not matter whether I believe him! What would I have done in his place? The naked truth is that I have no idea, but in any case, beyond and besides literature, you can't leave a friend all alone in such a terrible trouble. I pray for his luck to improve. Maybe prayer is stronger than literature!

25-26 November 2010

The Tour of Krakow in a Single Night, together with the Incredible and Banal Love Story of a Yankee Tourist

It is dedicated to her – previously, forever and now

It was around half an hour past midnight. The most spectacular and lengthy fireworks I'd ever seen had finished, I had put the photo camera in its protective holster and we were thinking about whether we should go home or maybe whether we should enter a *kawiarnia*, or rather a *piwnica*, for a last beer for her, a last glass of vodka for me. Or the reverse, because, after all, we are not any kind of dogmatists, although beer is more or less forbidden to me. Here, however,where I walk for hours on end, I sometimes breach the rule. After some very short deliberations, we opted for this last variant. Of course, as always, I would have preferred it to be a *piwnica*. I love madly the fact that here, in Krakow, I can go down the steep stairs into the stone entrails of the city, inside the caves made by the hand of man six hundred, four hundred, or only two hundred years before – these last being almost recent, almost contemporary, when compared to the others.

We went all around Rynek Główny, the great square, the central square. We also ventured a little onto the commercial streets that lead to Planty, the giant circular park which marks the former fortifications destroyed by the Austrians, but we did not find any open *piwnica* which was not playing host to the parties organised for New Year's celebrations. We had not booked places for such a thing because it seemed stupid to be tied to a certain spot for the whole night during the passage between years.

We always preferred, since we had started spending the New Year in Krakow – that is for some seven-eight years – to dine at home on what I would prepare like a grand master chef. Then we would drink a glass or two, take a leisurely walk towards the square, enter some local bar if it was too early, walk through the crowds and take photographs, finding, in advance, a good spot for the spectacle of the fireworks. Meanwhile we would warm ourselves from my metal flask – a gift from a very good female friend who gave it to me when she saw how much I envied another good friend. That is to say, we warmed ourselves with strong liquor if it was too cold outside, took pictures of the fireworks, embraced in the huddle, addressed to each other the appropriate best wishes, and finally went somewhere inside for the last glass, or the last glasses.

While we waited for the fireworks, we filled in our time watching a man of around fifty years of age who had arrived in front of us with a slightly staggering but decided walk, only to stop suddenly in front of the L'Occitane shop, across the road from the wall on which we leaned. Then he didn't move for almost a quarter of an hour, deep in thought, his eyes looking into the void, but directed almost imperceptibly upwards, completely abstracted from the context and indifferent to those who brushed past him while going one way or the other.

Taking advantage of his sovereign indifference, I actually photographed him, thinking he would be good to use as a character at some point. And look – he became one, a secondary character, it is true, although I haven't even transferred the photos from the laptop to the computer! At the moment we had advanced seriously with our most extravagant suppositions, he left rapidly towards the square, as suddenly as he had arrived, leaving us to hold our speculations in our arms; but just as I stole his image by stealth, I also had stolen his exploits!

When we had already started to get worried that we would not manage to find a proper place, we negotiated carefully about changing the possible and improbable *piwnica* for a *kawiarnia*, a coffeehouse, a beer hall, a *resto* above ground. Before the fireworks, we had seen, in our lazy wanderings, that near Rynek Mały, the small square behind the cathedral, they had opened the terraces of the public houses situated in the building of the former train station; that is, if we are talking about a train station here, and not about something else, because at this moment I can't remember precisely and I don't have the inclination to look for it in my countless guidebooks, albums and maps of the city. It was still pretty warm and we were tempted by the thought of sitting outside on a terrace, towards the morning of the day of the 1st of January, together with that motley and cheerful assortment of Krakowers and foreigners coming from all over the world in order to celebrate the New Year. We hurried our steps with a certain enthusiasm, turned the corner, passed by the well-guarded consular offices, reached the platform – even if it was not a train station, the thing is still a platform – with pubs and terraces arranged one near the other, and we saw that they were already turning the chairs over the tables! Some latecomers were finishing their drinks, the hasty waiters were gathering plates and glasses, and no more orders were being taken. Strange – so many people had come out into the town and they were already closing, although it was not one o'clock yet! Of course, we swore at them – and not just in my head – taking advantage of the fact that I could do it in the Romanian language. Me – with some enthusiasm; she, as befits someone who is almost a true Krakower, rather muted. But, getting over our anger, we nevertheless had a problem, as the president of the Senate of a banana republic with a temperate climate would say. Where should we finish the night of the passage between years before taking an orderly leave for our home and crumbling down into the sleep without dreams? Or with dreams, because we are not all that exclusive! Of course, we could have left to search for something that was open and free on the streets that were more distant from the centre, maybe even in our own neighbourhood, but this way we would have, more or less, ruined our ritual. We had always finished the exit from the last night of the year here, in the centre, even if it was in front of a shop that was still open until late after midnight in order to exhaust its stock of drinks.

Somewhat undecided, we stood in the middle of the road, and, feeling rather nervous, I had lit a cigarette when she said: "Maybe it's open at Karczma". Oh, yes! This was, in an approximate translation, "the boozer from Maricica's yard". It was, maybe, the most picturesque party location, in a kitsch style that was so crazy that it was almost beautiful, with a door in untreated wood on which the name and opening hours are written in red paint, with tables and chairs of strong wood, painted dark brown, and with a mix of unimaginably "folk-style" props. Everything was located on not more than fifty square metres of the ground floor, with another twenty on the upper floor, because a wooden staircase led to a sort of top level raised on a floor of beams and plank.

On top of the bar there were two mannequins, a man and a woman, dressed in traditional costumes from Małopolska, Lesser Poland. There was even a decorated Christmas tree which was pretty big, along with the toilet with a single cabin, which always had a queue, no matter how few the customers might have been – because, it seems, there were never few enough!

Yes, yes, yes, Karczma was the most appropriate place to end the night in town. I liked this place, as kitschy as it was, because it was welcoming and warm and it had always waited for us – when we did not find room somewhere else – with two free chairs or two wooden little benches.

Well, we decided the destination should be this, our old tavern, where you can eat the best smoked meats in the world, and we started hurrying towards it. On a nondescript wall, en passant, I noticed an inscription written in white paint, "Cracovia kurwa", oeuvre of some patriot from the League of Polish Families or from the Self-defence League, who was strongly set against the foreigners that haunt his city. He had nevertheless written the Latin name, not the Slavic name of the town. Another patriot replied at a distance of a few metres: "Cracovia pany".

113

They were both wrong, of course, because it is impossible to reduce Krakow to a single quality, it cannot be just a whore or just a lady! I can't say if the patriots had multiplied – or the reverse – from the integration onwards, because I had already encountered these polemical inscriptions on walls, on the pavement or on the wall facing the Vistula, even from the time of my first arrival here, around the middle of the last decade, in a different century and a different millennium. I had seen them; I had understood them without an interpreter and I had photographed them, I no longer know how many times, from the moment I had decided to capture the faces of Krakow, something which I didn't do on this particular occasion.

In the beginning, I thought they must hold a deep significance, but now they seem to me as superficial as the inscriptions that encourage the football team which, until a short time before I came on this new Krakow holiday, had a Romanian trainer. His name too was in the graffiti, but I did not have the curiosity to find out if it was well-meaning or not. In the end, I haven't come here to rediscover my motherland, and the messy and confused arguments from back there, but rather to escape a little from her loving, insistent and suffocating embrace.

That's an extra reason for not bringing with me the football obsessions of a visionary club owner, who is haunted by the angels of light and counselled by God Himself, twinned with those of a national president in a single block[32] of inspiration. Yes, it is very good to step out, every now and then, of that dizzying, hysterical and confused maelstrom

---

32 The author is here making a reference to Gigi Becali, owner of Steaua Bucharest Football Club, an extremely devout and colourful character, and the no less controversial President of Romania, Traian Băsescu.

which exhausts your time and energy, which squeezes you mercilessly as if you were a fruit, over-ripe with juice, and then throws you out among the countless husks, collateral victims of the transformation. It is also good to place, every now and then, the screen of distance between you and that crazy world, because it is only in this way that, after you look at it with lucidity, without illusions, you can still accept it, you can still meet it again with a certain understanding, and even with a drop of tenderness and affection. But I do not want to talk about this now, here...

I once read in a sociology textbook — or maybe it just seemed to me that I read it and I am remembering things which I had never actually read — some interesting things about social space-time and about the complexity of human interrelations. It was written there that, "physical" time is measurable, uniform and indifferent to our experience. On the other hand, the time lived by each one of us, by larger communities or by groups formed ad-hoc with a view to solving a problem or purely and simply to spend time together, is non-uniform, marked by our experiences, "coloured" — as Blaga, Vulcănescu or Vasile Băncilă [33] might say, and coming from a different perspective. Both the positivist sociologist, and his predecessors, gave the example of the celebration, that is space-time stolen away from work-time. Not like sleep or regular free time, but a space-time that behaves differently, and is strongly marked by subjectivity or by inter-subjectivity — in this latter case, the discourse being about social representations of time. During celebrations, time passes differently, of course; but the time of love also passes in other ways, the times of war or revolution pass in a different manner,

---

33 Romanian philosophers of the 20th century.

and so does the time of waiting.

We went through the narrow gangway, we arrived in front of the un-waxed wooden door, inscribed in red, and, even before opening it, we realised it must have been full – we could hear the music, we could perceive a mix of voices, smoke was coming slowly out through the spaces between the planks of the door. Nevertheless I pressed the door handle thinking we could, at least, cast an eye, steal an image.

It was full, some tens of people on a surface of some fifty square metres, but most of them standing, dancing – guests and staff all together, not just the waitresses but also the cook, who was dancing in a relatively sensual manner with one of his colleagues, and even the young and massive landlord who moved in a leisurely fashion with one of the waitresses. His fiancée sat on a tall chair at the bar, and sucked on a coloured drink through a straw, and watched the dancers without too much interest.

It was full fraternisation, as we could see, which had probably started around midnight. The place was full, but we saw a free table in the corner opposite the door, so we went over quickly and occupied it. The table was rather long, and there were no chairs but two wooden benches with backrests, on which four people would have been overcrowded, but where two could sit very comfortably. We took off our thick coats, and set them next to us, so they should be a sign that the table was taken, that we were still waiting for someone – because we were in the mood to feel somehow intimate in the hustle and bustle of the place. We had a table.

We lit our cigarettes, then we waited and waited until

we realised that, because of the dancing, our chances of receiving something to drink were very much reduced. Taking advantage of the stormy appearance of a youngster at the bar, she went over quickly, caught him just as he was getting ready to disappear again into the backroom, and managed to order Porter, a Polish black beer which is almost as good as Guinness – some Poles even maintain that it is better. I don't want to make distinctions, it is just as good. When she returned victorious – in fact, partially victorious, because we still had to wait some dances worth of time until the beer would arrive – we started to look around us, to fix the landscape, to take X-rays of the characters. We both felt that a story could be born out of all this celebratory atmosphere. We identified the regulars of the house, a few elegantly dressed old men who chatted around vodka or beer glasses. They were people with whom she'd had the chance to exchange some words on other occasions, and who, having adopted her, raised their glasses as a sign of cheers when we looked in their direction. We contented ourselves with inclining our heads, not having anything to raise in order to return the gesture of amiability.

Near them was a table with Orientals, two men and a woman, who seemed to be drinking soft drinks – in any case, something that seemed to be without alcohol – and who took photos every now and then, something which I was also going to do very soon. Near the staircase that led to the few tables upstairs, a group of Italians of various ages were huddled at a very small table. She had seen them there before and she had talked to them a few times – so we exchanged some greetings without having anything with which to make a toast. In the opposite corner, to the left of the door, there were some Russians, or at least this is what they seemed to be because of their language, since they spoke it quite loudly, their words somehow imprinting themselves in the smoke-filled air of the room at the moments when the music came to a short break between melodies.

There were other clients as well, whom I don't remember anymore. Anyway, the movement seemed to be continuous from the tables to the cluster of dancers, from one table to the other, from one group to another. The door opened a few more times, but since the Karczma seemed to have had its fill, only a young man came in, an Arab, or maybe a Greek by the appearances, who went to the upper floor, failed to find room there, stopped at the bar, where there was nobody, stayed a bit more and then left the way he came.

It was also written in the textbooks, or I just seem to remember that it would have been written in a book which I believed I'd read, that people behave differently in crowds, from various queues to the people gathered in a train station or an airport, on a beach or a stadium. It seems logical to me, and, anyway, this matter was discovered and explained some hundred years ago by Gustave Le Bon, in his celebrated text about the psychology of the masses. Nothing new, therefore, but something new was still there, somewhere – in the observation that I verified a posteriori that, in such a crowd, an unexpected event may intensify the complex interpersonal relations up to the level of explosions of violence, which can be seen with football games when a goal is cancelled, when there is a controversial event, a referee error etc. But it is not just this kind of violent, unpleasant event that happens, but also others, which are positive. If we stay with football here, I am referring to the cheers which accompany teams to victory, but things are the same with religious processions, with groups of soldiers who sing while marching, or with groups of wedding revellers or just purely and simply with party people. This is what I'd seen, on a giant scale, in Copenhagen, on a weekend when the Swedes come to buy drink more cheaply than in their country, which is flooded with super-taxation. We were about to enter such a space-time, one in which the complexity of human inter-relations was under pressure from the space-time of celebration ...

At the moment we had gone in, there was nobody at the round table near us, but it was nevertheless occupied. A short winter coat was placed on a chair, and facing the other chair there was a half-full glass, something more like a chalice, along with a bottle of champagne which was a little more than half full. While we looked around and appraised the public and the characters, the first two bottles of Porter arrived, brought by a tall, supple, very beautiful waitress, with whom she exchanged some words in Polish. The woman apologised for the delay, caused by the élan of the party which had enveloped all the people, so that it took a while until someone could get to the storage room to fetch the bottles.

She smiled while speaking and she really was beautiful. When she went away, she was stopped by a young man of up to thirty years of age, maybe a little over twenty-five, who had just entered the door – they were sort of the same age – and he had an athletic build, was dressed in a thin pretty pullover, in some sort of t-shirt, and had short-cropped hair. He kneaded nervously or impatiently an ash-grey beanie hat in one hand. They talked a little: he – precipitately, like the rhythm in which he was kneading the beanie hat; she – somehow at a loss, surprised, smiling, a little embarrassed.

She went to the bar, he took a seat at the table near us, raised the glass of champagne, emptied it and filled it again immediately. He then saw we were looking at him; he saluted us, raising his glass and said "happy new year" in English. As my English is good only for reading, she was the one who replied to him, but I also raised my glass. He turned his chair to face our table and, in some minutes, we found out he was American, his name was Thomas, he was a biology professor, he was in Krakow for some days, and he had fallen in love with Ewa, the beautiful girl who had served us and with whom he had talked a little while previously. If she will not marry him, he doesn't know what he might do! Anyway, he was not returning home, to his America, without her. We shook hands, we mentioned our Christian names in our turn and I asked her to translate for him my congratulations on his good taste in women. He laughed, but he didn't have the time to say anything, because the young landlord arrived at his table. He greeted the group, sat down and they started to talk. I don't think the English of the landlord was better than my spoken English, but they understood each other. Anyway, I understood Ewa would be free only at the end of opening hours, which would only be after the departure of the last client. While we amused ourselves with this light-headed love story, they continued their discussion about which we did not hear or understand a great deal more.

At any rate, when I was making reference to entering a specific space-time, which, on top of everything, is also marked by human clustering together, I did not think of unpleasant events first of all, maybe because I was also stimulated by alcohol consumption

– possibly a strong negative catalyst. I was thinking, instead, of events which are coloured in a positive manner, alcohol also being a factor which increases sociability and access to communication. We were about to go through two such events: the first was a calm one, warm and diffuse, which I would describe as affable hospitality due to an older character of impeccable civility. The other event – suspected, explored beforehand, smelled in the air, rather than fixed in an image, is connected to the stronger, more intense and even more superficial feelings of that possible young couple. My thoughts fly to Ewa and Thomas.

While we minded our own business, an older gentleman came in. He was elegantly dressed in a dark-coloured suit, with an unbuttoned grey overcoat on top and a hat that matched it. He went towards the bar and the group of dancers, shook hands, embraced people, kissed the women, then took off his overcoat and placed it on the bar top. A glass of champagne appeared from somewhere and he went amongst the tables to clink glasses, making the appropriate best wishes, and sitting to chat a bit more with the locals of the house. He was the true boss, the father of the young landlord. I whispered: "Here is the Godfather!".

He also exchanged some words with our enamoured American in English which was better than the son's, toasted with us as well, and then went up the stairs leading to the top floor. The American-Thomas-Professor-of-Biology emptied his chalice, stood up brusquely, without donning his winter coat and quickly went for the door, with his beanie hat in his hand. He went out at the moment when the Arab or Greek, the one who had come in before and then left, was just returning. We kept on discussing this love story which was being born or was maybe just finishing before truly starting, all under our eyes.

Ewa came from the neighbouring table, took away the bottle which still had enough champagne in it, took the empty chalice as well and placed a hot snack on the table, together with a big glass of beer. Maybe he'd ordered this when they talked earlier? Was it, perhaps, of her initiative? We could not tell, although it seemed a gesture full of attention and care. We appreciated it between us, and, smiling, also shared it with her. She replied with another smile. So we ordered two more Porters, which, this time around, were going to arrive much sooner, but not that soon. While she poured the beer into the glasses, she said to Ewa in Polish that "the boy risked getting tipsy" and that he had done well to go for a little to get some air outside.

I could not say from her tone or her words, which she translated after the girl went back to the bar, if there was any mutual interest between her and Thomas, or whether there was only the normal solicitude shown to a client of the place. The owner came down the stairs and invited the son's fiancée to dance, and the son invited Ewa, with whom he chatted while dancing. He spoke with detachment; she approved or disapproved only by lightly and elegantly moving her head.

Thomas returned, sat at the table and began eating the hot snack, without apparently being too convinced that he should do that. He ate about half, drank some mouthfuls of beer and watched Ewa dance. I could not tell how tipsy he was, but about being in love he needn't have said a word because one could see it from a distance of thousands of leagues. The truth is that anyone could have been in such danger from the first glimpse of Ewa, even more so a young man who had so little experience – as it seemed to me after the few words we had exchanged, but also taking into account everything I had noticed in the past two-almost three hours.

We ordered two more beers, which arrived in the usual rhythm of the night and which we drank quickly, following the evolution of the situation on the ground. Ewa changed the half warmed up beer for a fresh one, but in a small glass of 300 mils. While she stood near Thomas's table, he caught her discreetly by the hand, and she did not pull it back. Eventually we started to feel our fatigue and decided to leave. We donned our coats, waved at the people who could see our greeting, smiled at Ewa who was coming through the door behind the bar, and we left, arranging our clothes as we went. We squeezed through the door which was barely open – just enough as to let the smoke out and to permit the loss of the heat accumulated in the small and noisy neighbourhood bar and its frenetic gathering...

*

"How does it end, how will it end?" I asked her after we left the narrow and dark gangway for the wet flagstones of Rynek.

The square displayed the effects of the assault during the celebration of the passage between years – thousands of broken bottles, disposable cups, remains of the fireworks and firecrackers exploded during the night, beer cans, plastic bags, crumpled newspapers etc. But some tens of people wearing the insignia of the municipality's sanitation services, with dustcarts, sweeps, dustpans, and hoses connected to fire hydrants, had already started their general cleaning operation. The stage rose black and somehow incongruous, following all the noise it had sheltered in the middle of the lower side of the square, in front of the Sukiennice commercial galleries.

"I don't know. There are several possibilities, anyway. They have a short affair and he leaves. She falls in love with him as well, because at the moment she does not look in love, but only available, and the story gets longer. Or, nothing will happen, either definitively, or punctually even."

"Good, agreed; but what do you think? Is there no other possibility?"

"Which?"

"Well, he is tipsy, right? She is invited to dance either by the young landlord, or by the old one, or by the colleagues, maybe even by the clients. Let's suppose that, on the background of drink, he gets into a fit of jealousy, grows angry, makes a scandal, and it all ends up in fighting and so on."

"No, I don't think this will happen. The fact that he was restless from the moment we appeared there, in fact from before that time, because he was out when we came in, is not a sign of nervousness; nor is it one of jealousy, but of impatience. The man was waiting; he is waiting for the opening hours to end so he can talk to Ewa at length. For the moment, he is not even drunk, he is just a little tipsy, and Ewa is taking care that things don't develop otherwise. You saw that she took away the champagne bottle when it was only half empty, and the second beer she brought was a small one, as she had taken away the large glass when it was barely begun, under the pretext that it had grown warm..."

"Well, but why does she do this? Does she love him?"

"I don't know this, irrespective of how much of a woman I am. But I am certain she is interested in him, one way or another. I do not know how far, I do not know how much. But, from everything she did this night, from all the gestures, words, and even her silences, it is clear this is more than the normal care for a client... I think she is also testing him..."

"He answered the test well, up to now. Isn't it so? He didn't say a word, either when she disappeared with the bottle of champagne, or when she brought a small beer instead of the large one. He hardly ate anything, too..."

"Yes, he answered very well. Besides, he is a very cool kid, polite, nice, and on top of that he is in love like a teenager."

"Teenager?"

"Of course he is more than that age-wise, but this story does have its teenage exoticism, doesn't it? An American arrived only for a matter of days, he's probably seen her two or three times by now... This impatience he cannot hide, the way he kneads his beanie hat in his hands and especially his gaze – you've seen his eyes, after all!"

I nodded my head approvingly and we continued our way. On Szewska Street, the McDonald's was open and extra-full, people eating even in the street. I saw as many people at some kebab shops we passed along the road. The folks who realised that people will grow hungry after many hours of standing outside and drinking variable quantities of alcohol, were making beautiful money even at that hour, near morning time, when the skies had started slowly to grow lighter. Even the kebab shop at the entrance on Krupnicza was open, across the road from Teatr Bagatella. Some drunks – there were much fewer than some six-seven years previously, anyway – passed us by staggering, parting the groups temporarily.

A *góral* [34] who was well-dressed but in a somewhat jumbled manner, with branded shoes and a peasant girdle, made a remark about my hat and said to her that he needed a few more zloty as he had not drunk enough that night. He did not beg for it, mountain folk never beg anywhere, and even less over there; he had claimed the money in virtue of having praised my hat. I received permission to photograph him, and we gave him in exchange, all of us laughing, the small change in our pockets and then we lazily left for the house...

How might it have ended? Who knows. The next day, around lunchtime, I went out for a walk on my own, so that I could clear my mind after a sleep which had been pretty heavy and agitated, with moments when I surprised myself by having my eyes open. I had eaten too much when we reached home, I had drank a little too much over the night of celebration. On the Krupnicza there were still some small lost vestiges of the eruption overnight, with a bottle which had escaped the dustmen leaning on a wall, some items of clothing forgotten or thrown away, hanging by a door handle, a fence railing or tree branch. For a change, Szewska was perfect, cleansed like the interior of the hand. Just as in Rynek Główny, apart from some puddles of water, a sign that it had rained in the morning, you could not see anything but the flagstones.

I walked toward the Karczma "from Maricica's yard". I entered the gangway, trod lazily on it and, having reached the un-waxed wooden door, I found it was closed. Of course, people were probably still collapsed in the sleep of recuperation. I wanted to go out through the other end,

---

34 A Polish word which means "highlander"

towards the small square, but suddenly something hanging by a slat in the window's shutter drew my attention. In the semi-obscurity of the place I could tell from the first what it was. I went even closer, and touched the object which was soft to the touch and grey in colour. It was the beanie hat which Thomas had kneaded in his hands for a good part of the night. What had happened in the end, I wonder? I did not find an answer. But maybe she will, because I did not decree sole ownership of any subject we have lived and discussed together! I was just the first to bring it up when we woke, with heads that were a little too heavy, in the afternoon of that day of the beginning of the year.

I could not even have found an answer. I could not have found an answer simply from observing the deeds from outside, because, as it was written in that sociology textbook – or as I believed that I might have read in a sociology book about which I, perhaps, had the false memory of reading – at the moment when the space–time continuum meets in a privileged event, as in a sort of geometrical locus, with the complexity of human interrelations, anything might happen, absolutely anything, including – or maybe especially! – the magic, the grotesque, the sublime, the irreparable...

January – February 2007

What Was the German Looking for in Poland?

I cook rarely, very rarely, even. In the circumstances, I hurry to address warm greetings to the new gastronomic website of Boerescu, as well as to his guides to wines and various other fermented or distilled drinks. Not only because I eat daily, and – from time to time – I also drink, but because, among so many untiring agents of culturalisation, finally one was found to deal with civilising us. As the noble Paşadia, the man who knew the real Arnoteni, used to say: "neither the knife in your mouth, nor the fork in the fish".

No, I am not some adept of Spengler and I do not believe that, because of the process of civilising, our hoarfrost-like layer of culture would somehow go to hell. Furthermore, the West from where our Lights have come, and from where the light still arrives even now, that West has kept on waning for well over a hundred years, and it still hasn't disappeared yet! In the end, however, we are not talking in these pages about what, how, and how much I cook and eat – not only about this, anyway – but about the sole moments of joy, if not straightforward happiness, lived by a young German during the half year he spent, full of anxiety and difficulty, in the city which is, after all, one of the most beautiful in the world. I think his name was Michael, but even if his name were Hans or Otto I don't think the situation would have changed in any way, because I don't think there could be some predestination connected to one's name.

Michael was around twenty-five years of age, he had just finished his German language and literature studies in Berlin, the place where he hailed from, and had already arrived in Krakow for a few months, a little while before the start of the university year, as a lecturer in the Institute of German Studies of the University. He was tallish, thin, with brown eyes and light brown hair, so, speaking from the physical point of view, he was not quite a symbol or a monument of Germanic purity and toughness. I would meet him on the stairwell of the block where our flats were – his was situated right above mine – around the building – or in the shops around, and we greeted each other vaguely, bowing our heads and mumbling – me, a Polish or German formula of greeting, and he, invariably, a German one. We never talked, because he was hermetically fixated on his maternal language, which I frequent not just episodically, but also straight in a rhapsodic manner. It is true that I heard him a few times approximating formulae in French and Italian, but I would not bet important amounts on him as a translator to and from these languages. Michael, however, was not fixated only on his maternal language, but also, perhaps even more, on the image, remembrance, memory of his mother. His longing for her was pasted on his face as a stable melancholy, which to me evoked the distant Romantic poets of his homeland walking pensively and lazily, some two hundred years earlier, through the impenetrable German forests. He was also complaining, to those with whom he could make himself understood in one way or another, that he did not suffer from being so far away from his mother for such a length of time, and that he was not going to be in Krakow for long, although he had nothing against the city in itself.

He could even have said sincerely that he liked it very much. As he never evoked his father, I thought that this person must have disappeared in some manner or another from his life ages ago – that is, if he had ever been present, of course. In the end, a sort of typical case for the psychologists, a goldmine for the psychoanalysts: a single boy, raised only by the mother, and always restrained by the hand, a situation which causes dependencies that often exceed the normal. Still, it is not my business to perform psychoanalysis here and now, as it wasn't appropriate even back in that time to start doing some sort of psychotherapy. The only thing I could do for Michael, and this, from the very start, without even realising it, was to offer him a good meal, the best he had been fated to have in Krakow, maybe one of the best in his entire life as a single boy raised by a single mother who was, of course, careful and cautious to the point of hyper-protectiveness. Look, I can't help myself, I am starting to go with psychological clichés worth two coins a bag!

(So I cook rarely, very rarely. Maybe, for an average, around once every month and a bit, but almost never when I find myself in Romania. For a change, in Krakow I cook – I used to cook – several times a week. Not complicated things; let's say, beans, or cabbage with sausage and smoked meats, but not from the supermarket – from the market, from the *górali*. *Górali* come from *góra* – it is pronounced with an *u*, from which we have "Gura Humorului" in Romania – a word which means "highlanders". Or rice with mushrooms, with mushrooms again from the *górali*, and olives. Or other simple things, as simple as possible. Why do I almost never cook in Romania? Because, in kitchen-related activities, the state of mind is as important, if not even more important,

131

than the ingredients and the recipes. If somebody catches me cooking here, there is no doubt that I either feel too well, for strange reasons, or I might have gone completely mad. I am not talking about coffee or green tea, of course, which must flow in waves during the course of the day, and even of the night, which I always prepare in anticipation, so that I should never be caught out by penury.)

But let me set parentheses aside and go for the deeds! Among other things, in Krakow I never miss out on preparing the main course for the meal on New Year's night. And I am not talking about fish here, as per the Polish custom, but about meat. Red or white, but meat it should be. Irrespective of the fact that I opt for beef, pork, turkey or chicken, the recipe is kind of the same. Of course, for the chicken I will not make the marinade with red wine, but with beer, and for the pork with white wine. But these are matters which are known to almost everyone who has ever laid hands on a frying pan. We had chicken at the passage between the years I am talking about – but, and this should be clear, from the market, from the *górali*, not the pale-purple apparitions from the supermarket! So, I bought the chicken from the market on 30 December, and nearer to the evening I started to "work" on it. I washed it well, and I inserted apple-quarters, potato quarters and onion quarters in it. I inserted in the meat garlic cloves cut lengthways. Pay attention. Do not use a regular knife in order to make the holes in the meat, but rather one of the stiletto-type, or even a screwdriver which has been sterilised in advance, otherwise the chicken will "crack" in the oven and that is a pity. The chicken prepared like this was placed in a vessel, which should be taller, rather than wider, so that it would sit somehow leaning on the walls and with the incision facing upwards. Then I poured two bottles of beer until I covered the "victim". I added salt, pieces of apple, potato, mushrooms, garlic and all kinds of herbs, from the Mediterranean kind to basil and dill – for me, a recipe without herbs is barbarous, if not straightforward useless or even dangerous I added on top of that almost a centimetre of olive oil that would act like a lid. If I placed a real lid on it I did that rather as a protective measure. I allowed everything to sit there for some hours, then, upon going to bed, I placed the dish in the fridge. In the morning, the first thing I did, even before the first coffee and first cigarette, was to take out the dish and I leave it to sit at room temperature until the evening, when the time for the trial by fire came. I took the oven tray, buttered it – but, again, butter from the *górali*, not from the supermarket! – then I placed the chicken in the centre of the tray, poured the marinade on top, including the solid elements and all, and I placed the tray in the oven. The oven is electric, so you start cooking in increments of calorific powers until you get stable at 150. While the chicken – in fact, a true hen, as it was from the mountainside, wasn't it? – was baking, I prepared a generous *mujdei* garlic paste using some four bulbs. I don't know how you go about making your *mujdei*, but I recommend the more laborious but certain procedure of crushing the garlic cloves with a fork, after previously cutting each one into pieces. It works easier if you have rough salt at hand. Do not forget vinegar, use olive or rice oil and do not exaggerate with the water. It will come out exactly as it should, like at father's table, because with us this was the prerogative of the father! While I was grinding the *mujdei*, I kept casting an eye through the oven window, opening the door to baste the chicken with the marinade, plus other items and seasoning.

When the chicken was almost – I repeat, almost! – ready, I turned the oven off, I covered the *mujdei* pot with something and placed it in the fridge – if it stays for too long at room temperature, it gets a taste I don't like – we got dressed, I placed a bottle of Dalwhinnie in the bag – some 15-year old *single malt*, and we went to Rynek Główny, the Central Square, for the party of New Year celebration in the street. I won't say here how this goes because I have already recounted about the New Year street celebration in Krakow in "The Tour of Krakow in a Single Night, together with the Incredible and Banal Love Story of Yankee Tourist". Anyway, after the fireworks and the breaking of a bottle of champagne, which was rather bad, meaning Ukrainian and too sweet, we started lazily towards home. When we were some hundred metres from the foreign lecturers' block, we saw that on the floor above us the German and some other boys and girls were making enthusiastic gestures from the window, calling us there. We went up, we had a share of a Bacchic/enthusiastic welcome, but disillusion soon descended upon me. A multitude of beer bottles and banal vodka – not even Żubrówka! – but food-wise there were some little plastic plates full of peanuts and other vegetable dry goods, petit-fours, salty biscuits etc. A German New Year party? The thought is frightening! Confronted with the disaster that was as imminent as a *blitzkrieg*, I asked permission to go one floor down for a matter of moments. I took from the fridge whatever fell into my hand – "pork matters", but from the *górali*, this should be clear! – smoked salmon, *cașcaval* cheese, and even the sheeps' milk feta brought for a friend who had studied in Cluj and worked in the embassy here for some ten years, which is something that does not exist in their country, is not fabricated, and is not imported either! I added the three bottles of light, white wine from the Rhine, not something of a mysterious brand, but very pleasant, and, before climbing up with my offerings, I quickly restarted the electric oven. I set up the big cauldron for a generous *mămăligă* polenta. After I left all the necessaries for the start of the feast with them, I descended and watched over the chicken until it was as golden as it should be. Great care is necessary at the end if you don't want to let it "escape" to burning.

In a moment it was ready. Such a tremor, such commotion. I cannot find more appropriate words to evoke the welcome that was given me when I entered carrying in one hand the chicken on a platter, and another platter crowned by a golden and steaming *mămăliga* polenta in the other hand, with the hook of the vessel into which I had spooned the *mujdei* garlic paste gloriously hanging off a finger.

The welcomed like the welcoming, but you should have seen the appetite, although they had rather depleted the snacks brought less than half an hour earlier. I think that was the only time when I did not even manage to taste something that I had cooked. And I think it was the only time when I understood exactly what it means when they say that the cook gets full up from the smell alone. In a few minutes, everything was done, the German even gnawed on the bones – I think all of them! – and in the end he attacked the leftover *mujdei* only with *mămăligă*.

I sat down in an armchair and I sipped from what was left from my whisky bottle, which I had nevertheless protected, looking at them. A wonderful international spectacle, with exclamations in all the tongues of the earth in between greedy mouthfuls. The little Portuguese girl. The chatty Sandra. Ahmad, who had fought off cancer. Two Poles and a Polish woman. Or two Polish women and a Pole, because it is hard for me to remember precisely at this moment. Also Juan, who at some point played the guitar. I was watching the rustling of the small gathering with semi-open eyes, somehow from between my eyelashes, paying more attention to the rhythm of the ingurgitation rather than to the way in which it seemed that provisional couples were made and unmade, feeling more proud of my talent as a cook, rather than pushed forward by some voyeur instinct. Besides, this latter I had exhausted with extra measure at the hundreds of parties in which I had taken part from my adolescence onwards, whereas the pleasure of cooking was a very recent discovery. The only thing that caught my attention in the order of human relations was Michael, his head resting in the lap of the Brazilian lecturer, slightly past the noon of age, vaguely corpulent, but with curves that, at first sight, were still elastic; and I could not decide whether my German was tipsy, taking a siesta, or whether he was looking for a kind of compensatory consolation for the absence of his beloved mother.

The New Year party passed; my holiday was also finished after some more days and I left for home. After a little while, I received news that, no longer suffering the distance from his mother, after the massive and bronzed Brazilian lecturer had also left, the one on whose knees he was crying out every now and then his longing, and who was chased away by winter, my German, who was so adept at eating chicken with *mămăligă* and *mujdei*, had eventually also left for home. However the bad mouths in Berlin and elsewhere gossip that he had the habit of often going to the Television Tower in the former East Berlin, climbing in the lift to the restaurant on the topmost level, ordering there a salad, as vegetarian as possible, and then looking Eastwards at the horizon, his thoughts with the tastiest chicken with *mujdei* and *mămăligă* that he'd ever eaten. While he eats his salad, the aforementioned bad mouths say that he cries. He is eating and crying. He is eating, as somehow in the very popular poem which we learn from a very young age in school. Sometimes, in his better days, he imagines, with a happy smile apparently glued to his cheeks, that he is on a high, wide, floating flight over the dark romantic forests, over the wide Rhine plains, making a detour over the Masurian Lakes beyond the borders and then aiming South, towards Krakow. There I was again, in the city of my holidays, and I was looking at him, from my window, as he approached in his flight. Or, at least, this is how I imagine things, this is what I like to believe.

November 2010

A Very Good Morning for a Walk to the Beach

I had woken up, as I usually do here, at daybreak, so as to catch the kind sun which lasts for some two hours after the arrival of dawn. But, on that specific morning, after another long and exhausting day and a night shortened by dropping into the only old-style tavern in town, things were different.

The day had been long and exhausting because of the trip through the island's capital city with the pre-established aim of revisiting the grave of Kazantzakis, an aim which was accomplished, but also surpassed by revisiting the other few places worthy of being seen again. So, I had woken up with the night sitting on my head. I drank two milky *nesses,* instant coffees, one chasing the other, accompanied by a few cigarettes. I took an orange, which I peeled while descending the hotel stairs, my canvas bag with all beach necessaries hanging by my elbow: a towel, a book, a notebook, a biro, sun lotion, still water, chocolate and some oranges. The cigarettes, lighter, and the cigarette holder with silicon filters were kept in the deep pocket of the wide shirt, which seemed to be sewn on purpose for such eventualities. By the time I went out of the hotel door, the orange was already eaten, so I lit my cigarette for the road and started for the end of the little street leading to the main boulevard. It was, in fact, the only one, which also served as a national highway, running parallel to the motorway at the higher end of the little town, the one which was near the mountains. I had reached the boulevard in a matter of moments and I was trying to decide, with a mind which was not wholly awake, whether I should cross the road precisely in that spot where my little street met the boulevard at a right angle, or if I should cover some tens of metres more "on this embankment". As the traffic was calm enough, I decided to cross that way. Otherwise, this story would of course not have been born, not by the end of all the centuries and forever! Because everything depends on the most meaningless details, on those details which, being normally automatic, elude you, and pass unnoticed! So I crossed the boulevard and made my way up the street – to the east, in fact, because the difference in levels on the direction east-west is so small that you need to be very attentive, and even gifted, in order to perceive an up and a down – in order to reach one of my favourite little streets that led to the beach…

Yesterday, too, I had woken up with the night sitting on my head, not in order to go to the beach, but to catch the first bus for Heraklion. So, I wanted to see the town again, but especially to revisit the grave of Kazantzakis, to which he had been repatriated some decades after his departure for a better world. The world of the ancient gods, of Christ, of Buddha? Not even he could answer without a pause for thought. But it is definitely not the world of Lenin! I caught the bus and, after a little more than half an hour on the motorway dug in the island's rocks, I got off at the bus station, on the lower side of the town, some tens of metres from the Venetian harbour and from the new one, which in fact is connected to the old one. I started off under the sun that was already burning, towards the upper end of the town, where the grave was. Yet I was not in a hurry – but stopping here and there, photographing now the churches along the road, then the Venetian loggia, and further off the more elegant houses or the decrepit ones, some of them undergoing repairs, some seeming rather deserted. On a little street I stumbled upon a bar which was called "Jameson" and, in memory of London, I photographed myself with their sign above my head. Unfortunately it was closed, so I could not see it on the inside. I stopped, however, at a coffee house near the bazaar, I ate a pizza and drank a coffee, and then, crossing the bazaar with the photo camera always working, using my map and asking two passers-by and a taxi driver, I kept on getting closer to the grave, under the midday sun. Just like the first time, I was disturbed by the mix of grandeur and modesty of the holy place. The stone interior of the old Venetian fort was filled with earth, like a small mountain ending in a plateau. On the plateau, the thick, soft grass, almost elastic, and near the old walls an ample "border" of all the flowers, shrubs and trees of Crete. In the centre, a foundation some tens of square metres in surface made of white stone, on which sits the grave made of black stone blocks. A headstone made of limestone, on which the name is not even written, but only a quotation from the great writer on the front and, on the back, on a metal plaque, the word "peace" chiselled in several tongues, from Greek and Hebrew to English. A simple cross, made of two masts tied with sailing rope. I have never seen a grave more appropriate for a great writer, although I have visited several cemeteries up to now, from the Eternitatea *in Iași to* Bellu, Père Lachaise *and some London cemeteries. To the left of the grave, a little further off, from the time of 2004 there also rests Elena, his last wife, in a smaller and equally sombre eternal resting place. From the side of the plateau, beyond the sprawl of the town, you can see the great sea. From here, near to the grave, you can hear her ceaseless murmur. "Rest in peace, Fearless one…", I whispered while I headed for the stairs leading outside.*

I was walking on the pavement, my thoughts of the previous day's visit popping up pretty vaguely in my mind, which was still dizzy because of insufficient sleep. The sun had already started to warm up and I was looking for the shadow cast not by the trees, but by the awnings that stretched above every store, above every terrace. From the freshly sprayed pavements came a sort of coolness, and people were already getting busy, opening shops of all sorts. The town was waking up to a new day. That was the passage, the transition from quietness to the great agitation which was only going to stop late in the evening, late in the night. But some tales of the night-time peace were still preserved. I was walking lazily, perceiving this metamorphosis as through a kind of haze, when, suddenly, I stopped abruptly, almost with my mouth agape. On the terrace in front of a hotel, which was otherwise deserted, at a table that was almost glued to the glass wall, I saw a couple in a scene which was completely strange. I felt myself waking up all of a sudden, losing even the last vapours of yesterday, which had been gathered during the preceding night in the only old-style tavern on the west-side end of the town. He sat on one of the reed chairs, but turned with the back towards the little glass table with frame and legs also made of reed. She was seated, somehow crouching in front of him, almost on her knees, and she held his right hand in her hands. From time to time, she brought her lips closer, and kissed his hand. He was talking calmly, her tears flowed and she said nothing. The man was around sixty years of age, and she was some fifteen-twenty years younger than him, both of them were beautiful, still preserving well the traces of the beauty from their youth. They were blond, the Nordic type. He was almost greying, but, keeping in mind the scene in which I noticed them, I automatically told myself that they must be Russians, or Slavic in some way, because with other nations you do not actually see women kissing the hands of men. I was looking at them somehow hypnotised, and all sorts of hypotheses stumbled over each other in my mind, but I was not at all afraid of disturbing them, or afraid that they would notice my lack of discretion. Why am I saying lack of discretion. I was standing there with my eyes wide open, gawping! I was convinced, anyway, that they saw nothing around them, that they were totally caught in that drama which, I don't know why, I was trying to understand, to explain to myself. I was trying, but I didn't succeed, just as I don't succeed even now, although I also have the distance of time at my disposal, and my mind is much clearer than it was that summer morning I can only suppose that it was a question of love or death, even of love and death together, but I do not think I can say more than that. If I were one of those 19th Century writers of the omniscient type, as narratologists call them, the kind who know everything about their characters, from the details of marital status to the most intimate thoughts, this would be simple; but I am not such a writer. It would be just as simple if I were a writer of police novels, because I would give five Euros to the man at the reception desk and I would find out the basic details of the characters; then I would place a microphone somewhere at their table and I would listen in to their conversation. However, as I am not an author of police novels, this possibility also fails, and as I have no longer been a true romantic for a long time now, neither can I hang on to the beautiful, refined, and shattering speculations from the end of the 18th Century. As a consequence, I left their story to indecision, a real indecision, not one I was acting out, and I started again on my way to the beach. As I went I felt the haze, the vapours as dense as cotton-wool, due to the culinary and Bacchic session of the previous evening, settle back in my mind…

Maybe, after that long and exhausting day, I should not have stopped at the only old-style tavern in Hersonissos, or at least not have taken so much advantage of the hosts' hospitality. But, passing it by on the bus, I saw for the first time that it was less busy than when I usually made my way around. There were only some five people seated at two tables pushed together. They were locals, to judge by appearances, pretty well caught up in their party, while, at the entrance was a tourist couple who seemed to be finishing their orange juices. This is why I came off the bus at the following stop and made my way to the tavern. I went in and ordered a raki – since I had entered a traditional boozer, I should at least order something traditional. I don't know what happened. Either because I had used some Greek words from the few that I knew, or because I had set a manual of New Greek on the table, or because I had ordered raki, but after some minutes the landlord, whom I had seen talking with the folks at the locals' table, arrived with a platter full of slices of fried lamb and pizza slices, and another round of raki. At the Greeks' table there were four older and relatively decrepit individuals, and a man around fifty years of age, with black locks and a beautiful beard, as black as his hair. He seemed taller than the majority of the islanders and he was more elegantly dressed than his tablemates. I worked out, as best as I could, that my meal and the raki were a gift from that group of people. I looked at them and, as the one that seemed to be the chief was looking at me, I raised my glass in a sign of a toast and I saluted – or thanked? – them by lowering my head. He answered in the same way, after which he continued his discussions with his tablemates. Maybe he was the owner. I don't know. I could not get this any clearer. While I was eating, I looked at the old furniture, at the walls painted with the roller – like they used to do in our country in the older days – at the old decorative objects, some of them very old indeed: icons, maps, paintings, a bronze clock and other things which I can no longer remember. Only the television set, a giant plasma screen, set at the left side of the bar, on which one could see scenes from a football match, as well as the utensils specific to the kitchen and bar, made for a contrast with the rest of the furniture by their newness and modernity. While I was eating, the tall dark-haired man rose from the table, passed by my table, saluted me nodding his head and then went out. One by one, during the next few minutes, the others also left. The tourists had left without me noticing them. I felt good, ready to take a walk towards the hotel. I called the landlord so as to pay him, but he did not want to take any money from me, not even for the first round of raki I had ordered. I tried to reason with him in my inimitable mixture of Greek, French and English, but there was no way out of it. I then ordered another raki and a coffee – not an espresso, but a Greek one, made over sand, the sort you have to re-baptise in Turkey as being a Turkish coffee if you are not in a mood for discussions! I drank the raki quickly and the coffee at length, smoking two cigarettes, one following the other. I managed to pay for this order at least, rounding it up a little so that an appropriate tip would come out of it. My parting with the landlord involved us bowing at each other – so I won't talk about rope in the house of the hanged by mentioning "salam aleikum" – but only after I finished my activity as a photographer as well, capturing him in a portrait and in a kind of landscape shot with the most crowded wall as a backdrop. I made my way to the hotel, with the clear sensation that the last raki had been somewhat over the limits... I had also had a glass of wine for my meal in Heraklion and a small bottle of ouzo at the grave of Kazantzakis.

At some fifty metres from the place where I had left my two Slavic people with their mysterious drama and proceeded to the beach, I made a turn to the left and saw the sea from a distance. I walked on a terrace, then went through a side of the private beach with a pool which belonged to a hotel to reach the beach that was wide and public, and had more stones than sand. I veered to the right, towards my stone island which was separated from the great island by around a metre of water. My sight started to clear up, and I took my glasses off, hanging them from the pocket of the wide, sand-coloured shirt. As soon as I raised my eyes, I noticed there were two intruders on my island: a young man and a young woman. Cohabitation? The little island is pretty big, some twenty-something metres in length, with an average width of three-four metres. But the surface is not equally smooth everywhere on it, and the places on which you can sit in accommodation with others are pretty sparse. In that case, a conflict instead? Still, by nature, I am not a conflict junkie, and with the passage of the years my potential for conflict kept on diminishing. Should I change my place? No, I am not doing anything like that, you don't do anything like that. However, it is the first time in more than ten days, given that I've been coming here twice a day, that something like this has happened to me. I always found my little island deserted, which is why I designated it as being mine. Maybe it is better to return to the hotel and get more of the sleep I need...

December 2010

The Unexpected Appearance of Poseidon on the Island of Zeus

I was just approaching the end of the first half of my stay in Crete. It was in the afternoon around five o'clock, and my things had been left on the little island separated from the rockface of the giant island by around a metre and a half of water. I was diving, watching the shoals of fish of all colours, my thoughts pervaded by a faint echo of regret for the disappearance of my underwater camera at the hands of a thief in Prague. Suddenly, as I was raising my head out of the water in order to breathe properly, my gaze locked on a human apparition who was so spectacular, so suggestive, that I only just stopped the shout that had started to form at the back of my throat – Poseidon! It seemed to me that he looked so much like the ancient god of waters – well, like my mental image of him.

Some twenty metres away from me, on the rocky shore, a man around sixty years of age, wonderfully preserved, was just getting ready to descend to the sea. Of medium height, relatively massive, but with muscles that were still well outlined on his body– due in equal measure to nature and the sun, with a white beard that was long enough as to flutter in the breeze and hair which was just as white, but tied at the back of the head in an ample ponytail – he really was an apparition, an epiphany. Some metres away from him, a poodle that shared somehow the colours of the owner, white with some black spots, was barking playfully, friendly.

The old god of the sea descended into the water and started swimming decidedly, in a perfect *crawl* style, towards the wider waters. The dog climbed down to the seashore, dipped himself a little in the water, shook energetically then started to run on the shore in all directions, barking every now and then in the direction of his master, but not with much conviction. In the meantime, I also came out of the water, dried myself and took up *Report to El Greco* by Kazantzakis, which I had decided to re-read. Deep in reading, I did not manage to notice the return of the god from the waters, nor his departure. When I stopped reading in order to light a cigarette, I noticed that neither the poodle, nor the little mound made of the swimmer's clothes were there. You couldn't see any trace of the two comrades somewhere else around, either.

Every evening after dinner I am in the habit of going out for a longer walk on the seashore. When I feel a little lazier or too tired because of the sunbathing and swimming during the day, I choose the shortest road to a small breakwater to the east of the resort. I stretch myself on a lounger – a thing that I would not do in any guise during the day time, when I prefer the stone of my little island, and I look at the stars or at the waves, alternating peacefully the marine aerosols with those from the cigarette smoke. I sip from time to time a mouthful of whisky from a little fifty millilitre bottle. Of course, the little bottle originally held ouzo, but I prefer a drier drink, without sugar. Less often, but more energetically, I also take a mouthful of Crete's still water. Normally I do not feel too tired, so I choose the walk on the esplanade which is a few kilometres long, down to the little church from the harbour of Hersonissos. At the end of the road, I enter the church which is one third dug in the rock and two thirds built in stone. I collect myself for some minutes. I light some candles for the living and the dead, then I install myself on a wooden bench to the left of the church, under a cypress. But that evening I had noticed from a distance, with some irritation, that the little bench was occupied, so I continued my walk on the long breakwater that shelters the harbour and ends in a small lighthouse with a green but very strong light. Evening in and evening out, hundreds of little fishing boats, yachts, barges and even simple larger motorboats rest there and it is pleasant to hear the clinking caused by their rolling on the water and the bangs given them by the buoys. A sound which is more muted, in the end, than the one I heard another summer night somewhere further north, in a harbour at the North Sea. Suddenly, from a certain distance, I noticed that my favourite bench was free again, so I started vigorously towards the stone steps which lead to the church. I threw my canvas bag on the bench while walking, as a sign it was taken, and then I stepped inside the holy place for my short ritual of recollection and commemoration. I like to find myself alone in a house of the Lord, just as there are many other places where I like to be alone. I went out then, sat on the bench, prepared my cigarettes and the 50 ml little bottle of whisky, then rifled through the bag for the water bottle.

While I was doing all this, I was thinking of the rainbow that had appeared over the sea after a sunny rain that had not lasted even five minutes. I had admired it from the balcony of the room, while savouring my coffee after the noon meal.

An interesting phenomenon, the greater part of the sky was sunny, some ash-grey and compact clouds, some others that were white and lint-looking, so it was hard to ascertain from where the rapid, short and somewhat rhythmic rain had come, and why the rainbow had appeared while the last drops of waters were still falling.

Suddenly I heard the rattle of a motorcycle from the alley that climbed to the little church on top of the quay. It stopped in front of the church and, when I lifted my gaze, I saw my god of the afternoon getting off a scooter in the same time, more or less, as the poodle that had been sitting on the machine. While Poseidon parked the scooter, the dog made a circuit in the church, came out, and sat under a cypress tree in front of it. The man also went in, stayed some minutes, came out and locked the door. He saw me and greeted me by nodding his head and muttering something which I did not hear clearly and which I failed to understand. I replied to the greeting and he came closer. He saw the little bottle and he said, in English, that it was too small. I gestured to him to help himself. He took a mouthful and gave the bottle to me. It was gone very fast. He gestured to me to stay calm and he went inside the church. I was watching the small waves breaking on the shore inside the harbour but, instead, I heard those from behind the breakwater, which I could in no way see. Poseidon lingered for some minutes inside the church and returned with a half-litre bottle of raki and two small glasses. "Raki", he said, setting the bottle on the bench. I replied to him that in my language it is called "rachiu", which meant we had borrowed from them, if not necessarily the recipe of the product, at least the name. We stayed together for about an hour, chatting in the most bizarre mix of languages possible, and finishing the bottle. He was seventy-two years of age, and he had been a priest there for over thirty years. Before that, he had been a ship's captain. He had lost his first wife while he was at sea, when he was returning from a long trip from South America. The appetite for travelling passed and he joined, around the age of thirty-five, the theology seminary on the mainland. He served in the beginning in Crete's villages, but when it was possible, more than twenty years previously, he had settled there, in the church carved in the rock, two steps away from the sea. He conducted services according to the rule, but for the rest he was used to leave the church open, under the guardianship of God. It was only for some three years, in the wake of small thefts and damages caused by those who had started to shelter there for the night, that he had started to come in order to lock it when midnight got closer. He lost his second wife as well, but at least this time he was home, beside her, assisting in her long agony and watching over her demise. He was recounting his life peacefully, in the mix of languages which we had reached together, me – rather more in French, he – rather more in English, but we understood each other quite well; he was at peace with the world, with himself, and with the Lord on High. He saw the bag with the small reproduction on wood of an icon which was famous in Greece, that of Saint Demetrius, the father's patron saint, and he asked me whether I would like him to bless it. I did want that, of course. I don't realise why he felt the need to make his confession to me; maybe because I was a stranger – the Stranger.

We drank the last glass, we shook hands wishing each other *kali nichta*, and he went to his scooter. Before he

153

had reached it, the poodle, which had disappeared from my attention span, was already sitting on the small carrier, wagging its tail. He started the engine, saluted me in navy style this time, and departed down the alley, leaving in his wake the increasingly faint sounds of his machine and the happy barking of the dog. I stayed there, sitting on the little bench under the foliage of the cypress. I smoked another cigarette, two – even, then I stood up from the bench and wound my way lazily to the hotel. I was thinking that I had to wake up very early for the next day's planned visit to the cave where Zeus had been born. Still – what an interesting affair! To meet Poseidon under the guise of a servant of Christ! On the island of Zeus.

August 2010

A Nondescript President

One nondescript morning, a nondescript president of a nondescript country suddenly woke up. Suddenly and rather early, compared to how much sleep he would have needed after an evening and a good part of the night spent around several bottles of whisky of a quality which was almost very good, together with his miserly beanpole of a premier, the little man from External Affairs and the boys who headed the various special services that had bloomed like the lilac in springtime from the start of his first mandate. This event had taken place a good while ago, not even he could manage to keep track of his numberless mandates. So, he had woken up suddenly, earlier than normal, and with a strange an unpleasant sensation, that he reeked strongly of crap. In the beginning, he thought that his sphincter had let him down because of the liquor that had arrived from Scotland on a special plane, but he looked at his pyjama, kicked the duvet to one side, inspected the sheets closely and nothing – everything was clean, of a sparkling white, and only some creases disturbed the landscape. And yet, the smell of shit twisted his nose! He rose from the bed with difficulty, searched around the room, looked under armchairs, under some low tables, and even under the bed. He opened one by one the five doors of the giant wardrobe, then looked inside the massive *secretaire*, in a small closet where he usually kept his bottles hidden from his vigilant wife – and nothing. The doors from the bathroom and toilet of the bedroom were sealed shut. He nevertheless opened them, searched in the two intimate rooms, but nothing. He did not understand what the heck was happening. He opened the two windows wide, despite the pretty serious frozen conditions outside, left them open for a good few minutes but did not notice any odoriferous change around him. In the end, he accepted it. That strong smell, so nauseating that it turned your guts inside out, was coming from himself, from his own being. It was his personal smell, which had appeared by some maleficent miracle at the surface of his being. His heart started to beat powerfully. He sat on a chair, after taking a bottle of whisky from the closet and swigging some large mouthfuls straight from the neck of the bottle. He felt panic enveloping him, so he made an effort, stood up from his chair and directed himself to the bathroom. He threw the white, silk pyjamas in a basket for dirty laundry, although he had only worn it for the little bit of night during which he had managed to sleep. He entered the bathtub, started the appropriately warm shower, a little over body temperature, smeared himself with balsam, took a rough sponge, the sea-kind, and rubbed himself from head to toe, several times. He felt the scent of plants from the gel, but running through this he also felt the smell of crap as strongly. He put the stopper in and turned the water on, allowing it to run in the tub, then released bath mousse, sea salts and whatever seemed fit from what he had at hand. Sitting down, he rubbed himself again with the sponge soaked in balsam on all sides. The water seemed to mute the smell a little, but when he stood up and got out of the tub, wiping himself with a giant white towel, he felt his nose twisting. He knew that a body can start to smell like that, but only if it is dead for some time – whereas he was as alive as possible!

Once returned to his room, he took from a shelf a strong deodorant and sprinkled himself all over the body, then rubbed his cheeks, throat and the upper part of the body with a cologne that was just as strong. Nothing. He got dressed resignedly, looked at the pendulum clock and saw that just half an hour was left to the time he had to make an entrance at his office, under the scared gaze of the chief of cabinet. This was the ritual. When he was at the official residence, he entered the office door at eight o'clock sharp, under the scared gaze of the aide-de-camp – this was already the fifth or sixth one from the start of his first mandate onwards. He looked at himself in the giant mirror hanging on one of the wardrobe doors, holding his nose with his fingers. This was strange: although it was his own smell, he could not get used to it! He then went out, starting into the small and stylish hall where he sipped the first coffee of the day together with the wife. When he opened the door, he only heard her screaming "Lord!…" and saw her falling down, in a faint. He left her in the care of the serving girl and started to the official side of the residence, to the work cabinet of the president, the little one, because there was another one who was bigger, the fatherland! On his way there, he remembered that, after the boys had left, he had spent a little time in the retreat room near the office with his beautiful and brunette political counsellor. He opened the door of the retreat, saw her beautiful and naked in the white bedding, with a sheet that did not cover her ankles, with her long hair spread artistically over the pillow. Either from the noise of the door or from the smell that accompanied the president without abating, she woke up. While she raised up from the pillow, she let a "What the devil can stink like this…" fly. Her eyes encountered him, she opened them immensely wide, then closed them, opened them again, said "Am I dreaming, what the devil?", then thrust her nose in the pillow and stayed there without moving, her beautifully curved back up.

He left the beautiful counsellor to her own devices and continued his way down the corridor, to the main door of the office, although he could have done it straight through the retreat room. But he had never done that in the morning, from the start of the first of his mandates – all constitutional, of course, as he had changed the constitution I don't know how many times, according to the number of mandates that had to be supported by it. There were probably only some two colleagues, in eastern satrapies, who had enjoyed such long-distance lordships. One of them had started, even before him, to modify the constitution so that he could re-elect himself as many times he felt like it. The other one had amused himself even more with playing at democracy and had found some sort of puppet with whom he alternated at the helm of the state once every two mandates. When he was not in this posture, he was resting in that of the premier.

The president entered the office. The chief of cabinet looked at him scared, as per the rule, but the rule went off the hinges after this – he started to stagger, to mutter almost with froth in the mouth, he was near to fainting but managed to contain it, so that, after a last horrified look thrown at the president, he left the office slamming the door, and burst into running in so decided a manner that I am afraid he hasn't stopped, not even now, after such a long and bitter time.

On that morning, nondescript but so full of the unforeseeable, a nondescript president of a nondescript country was left alone in his office, without a chief of cabinet, without anyone else. He went and opened the windows wide, but no effect coming from it was felt inside the office. For a change, outside, in their decorative garrets, the soldiers on guard felt like being taken by fainting. The gardener, who was some tens of metres away from the windows, fell as if cut down with a scythe, and some drivers urgently entered their cars, closed the doors and started to smoke, a thing which they had never done before, since it was drastically forbidden by the regulations. Only the president could light a cigarette in the official cars. This latter, left alone in his office, sat down on one of the armchairs reserved for the guests and tried to understand what was going on, what was going on with him. He recalled that at the start of his mandates he'd had a philosopher as a counsellor, with whom he had parted when he'd had to choose between this one and the blonde political counsellor from back then. By the time he had managed to get rid of him, the counsellor had nevertheless filled his ears, even his mind, with all kind of stories about existence and essence, substance and form, matter and spirit and many others. Maybe the philosopher was not exactly mad, he said to himself in his mind. He sat for some more minutes with his head in his hands and, when he lifted his gaze, he saw that it had been one hour since he had arrived in the office. It was almost nine o'clock. Noticing that the opening of the windows had not solved a thing about the tragic olfactory issue, he stood up, went over and closed them. He then drew the heavy, massive garnet-coloured and gold curtains. Turning to the desk, he said to himself, in a whispered voice, that existence and essence must be set in accordance, if not the substance with the form.

He reached the desk, sat on the official chair, something between an armchair and a throne, opened a drawer with his left hand, and with the right he took an officer's revolver, black with ivory inlay, of the parade-type. The pendulum clock showed 9 sharp. It was 31 December in the year twenty-twenty... and something. He placed the revolver's barrel to his temple and he pulled the trigger. Almost at the same time as the blood and brains, an unearthly smell of roses, bay-leaf and myrrh started to rise from his body, and, floating out of the almost hermetically closed room, it rose above the conurbation, giving the good news to the Capital City of a nondescript country...

26 December 2010

Report on Two Couples Uprooted from Reality, Accompanied by a Vague, Imprecise Commentary Regarding Reality as Such

I don't know what came over me during that changing summer, which could also be this summer, but it just crossed my mind that I should start writing a novel. A realist novel. In fact, more than a novel which would respect the conventions of realism, but one that would be inspired straight from reality, meaning that it should borrow from life its characters and, as far as that was possible, their stories. Then, the problem of documentation was posed – it is posed. If we are talking about characters uprooted from reality, of course you need to lift yourself from your desk, get dressed, open the door wide and barge in. This is what I did, and I began by putting on a new vest under my light, summer clothes: with a t-shirt, short trousers and flip-flops, a canvas bag hanging on my shoulder with all the necessaries – a big towel for the beach, a spray for solar protection, a bottle of green tea, mint, cactus flowers, etc, taken from the refrigerator, the latest book by Henry Miller in translation, the one on the world of sex, two of the three satirical magazines, a pack of sugar-free biscuits, cigarettes, lighter etc, and I directed myself with elastic steps to the new lido in my neighbourhood.

I was haunted by the thought that, for a novelist, reality

is constituted especially by people and their events, and where the devil can you find reality more concentrated, and even huddled together, than on a beach, on a hot August day? Well, yes, I can say that I found a place chock-a-block with reality, starting with the entrance to the lido, where I queued in a line some twelve to fifteen people long! And when I eventually managed to enter the premises, I can say that I energetically hit reality face to face. I took one of the pathways that led to the beach. I reached the surface covered in fine sand brought from I don't know where. I squeezed as well as I could between the sheets heaving with naked bodies of both sexes, and even of an uncertain sex, as well as of all dimensions. I noticed a place with grass at the edge of the sandy surface which seemed good as a point for the observation of reality. I reached there, I laid down the big, plushy towel I had bought some two years previously in Crete. I undressed to the red vest bought from Decathlon. I stretched out, lit a cigarette and closed my eyes a little in order to clarify to some extent the gaze which had just passed from myopia to the reverse disorder, from minus to plus, as it were. Yes, I had chosen the right option! Where can you find more reality than at the lido? Human reality, the only one which is interesting for a novelist; reality, as the popular dictum would say, both on horseback and on foot, both dressed and undressed. I smoked with my eyes closed, and when I finished the cigarette I placed the butt in a tin I had brought for the purpose, because I am annoyed by the tons of rubbish of all sorts which gather in such a place on a beach day, although it teems with over one hundred classic rubbish bins and some tens of plastic bins of large dimensions. In the end – with the exception of myself, although in my case there is also at work a desire to not disturb excessively the environment in which I decided to observe reality – the only ones acting by the rules of good manners when it comes to refuse are the "Italians", the generic name for Romanians who are working abroad and are on holiday here. Also that man who is slightly older than I am, very tanned and with white hair, who I've seen here for some three summers already and with whom I exchange some words from time to time. Not even he used to be so careful, until one summer when he was visited by the two daughters who had left some ten years previously to wherever their eyes could see, one to Spain, the other all the way to Costa Rica, where she managed to open a medical physiotherapy practice. I was just thinking – I am thinking – whether I should not construct some kind of collective negative character from this immense group of misery-inducing, miserable, and rubbishy people, like a sort of ancient chorus that would accompany, for the length of my novel, the actions of the protagonists. On the other hand, I am thinking that I would be doing them too great an honour. I would do better writing a satirical, unmasking, article about them for some newspaper.

But enough with the palaver! I have not come here to outline the philosophy of characters, whether individual or collective, positive or negative or even neutral, and of both sexes, as it were. I have come here to observe reality in its concentrated and pure state. To work! I took with me the latest edition of *Cațavencii* and I started to look around attentively over the edge of the newspaper. I have to say that, since the *Academia Cațavencu* magazine became three, multiplying by schizogenesis, I have read two of the publications, *Kamikaze* and *Cațavencii*, abandoning precisely the first of them which had appeared, but which unfortunately ended up in the wrong hands, and, besides the strictly formal characteristics, does not inherit a thing from the formula used successfully for almost twenty years. Whereas an *Academia Cațavencu* which appears to be the same, graphically speaking, but in which you will no longer find the humour, not even if you search for it with the people's militia, is unreadable. Perhaps not even the two successors are on the same level as the old magazine, but they certainly have humour and you have something to read in them, although probably not from cover to cover, as things used to be up to the occasion of the first split, the one that happened a year and a bit ago.

Nevertheless, I said I was going to put myself to work and I see that I keep on with the diversions – this time about the state of the humour among the Romanians. My thoughts were also touched by the masthead of *Le Canard Enchainé*, among other national publications in the Latin category. So, I was gazing over the edge of the magazine while I pretended to be absorbed by reading. In order to hide the direction of my gaze, I had put on my sunglasses with the darkest lenses of the few pairs I owned. Travelling with my gaze, above the people and among them, somewhere at a distance of some eight-ten metres away from me, but on the sand, not on some patch of grass, my attention was attracted by a couple who I judged, even at first sight, to lack symmetry. They sat on two big towels, bigger than mine, his being blue to ultramarine, hers a sort of pale blue, matching, in different nuances of the same fundamental colour. She was beautiful, truly beautiful. The black hair, I don't know if naturally so, but if it was dyed, she used dye of a very high quality, and she had the attractive body of a *fausse maigre*, a false-skinny woman. If she had been dressed, I would have bet that she was too skinny, but as things were you could see some exceptionally arranged curves. She was without a bra, lounging face down, but one could still see one of the hardened nipples. Green eyes, which you should never trust – as the folk saying goes.

Speaking frankly, I liked her pretty much as a woman, as an animal – as misogynists say; but I am no such thing, so I liked her as a woman. Maybe, by contrast, he seemed even more banal and placid than he was in reality, in the reality from which I proposed to myself to uproot him, to uproot them both. Also around thirty years of age, he had mousy hair, skin which was too white, and eyes of an imprecise colour, oscillating from grey to light blue and green to yellow, although he did not seem to have problems with his liver. He had probably had, not a long time ago, a body which was rather athletic, but now his belly had become imposing– the belly of a beer drinker, because I believe it proper to mention the cause, the former muscles covered by layers of fat which were not very thick, but visible from afar. It was the appearance of a clerk of superior rank, a bank branch manager, or a director of an insurance company. I see that I had noted this down in a hurry about that first couple submitted to observation, almost in a stenographical manner, on some kind of schedule of characters. Further down, after a space I had left free, I had noted down: "There are nine out of ten chances that this cool chick cheats on him". Well. I left this couple to their own devices and turned my gaze round for some 45 degrees to the left. Some two metres farther off, depth-wise in relation to the first couple, my attention was attracted by another couple – again, asymmetrical, but in the opposite way, if I may say so. He was a kind of Apollo around forty years of age, around one metre and eighty-five centimetres tall, with beautifully drawn muscles under the tanned, almost olive skin. Not the deformed muscles of a body-builder, but somehow natural. His eyes were of an intense blue, "like two mountain lakes", as the chorus from a TV soap of the 1990s said. The hair was dark in colour and cropped very short, with a kind of a Roman fringe. He was – he is – what is called a man after whom women turn their heads in the street, not just at the beach. They both sat on a big sheet of an almost blinding white colour – she chose it, certainly, I said to myself and noted it down on the schedule, she chose it for the contrast. I cannot say that she was – she is – ugly, but I would be certainly exaggerating if I said beautiful. Regular features, naturally blonde to red hair, a well-proportioned body. What was – what is – missing? I think it was the sex-appeal, the brilliance without which beauty is not truly beauty, irrespective of the correctness of traits and shapes. This time, after the space I had left free, I noted down: "This boy jumps from bed to bed. Like a grasshopper. Like a male dragonfly". Full stop.

I admit it. I usually lie to my readers and, as much as this is possible, I try to lie to them beautifully. I invent characters starting with a strange nose, or the movement of a woman's bottom, then I embroider stories around them according to how my imagination runs. And I always try to instil an air of implacability, things cannot be otherwise but like this, an air of authenticity. But this time I want to be as honest as possible with my readers. I proposed to uproot the characters straight from reality and to try to reconstitute their story from real facts, to limit my imagination as much as I can. What if my observations, and especially the conclusions drawn from them, are incorrect? They certainly are superficial, anyway. I took my phone from the pocket of the short trousers, after I took them from the canvas bag, and I dialled Max's number. I told him that I needed his help and that of his boys, on the spot, and that I was at the lido in my neighbourhood. As if there were any other lidos! He replied that he was going to get in a car with two boys and they would be coming immediately. Max, in fact Maxim Dîrjan, is the owner of the first private detective agency to appear in town, about a year after the revolution. He says that "before" he used to be a militia officer, in criminal investigations, but I am almost certain he had been a *securist*, a member of the *Securitate* secret police. But this no longer matters nowadays, four five-year plans after the "events". I got to be friends with him, if I may use this term, some four years previously, when I wanted to write a novel with a police procedural frame and I deemed it necessary to do a little research on the field. I talked to some policemen I had met during the times I occupied a kind of dignitary position in this conurbation, but they did not tell me a great deal, they believed too strongly that the things appertaining to their job were secret. One of them recommended Max, according to the principle that a private detective is freer with his mouth than a detective in the public service. This is how things were. Not only did he tell me a multitude of general and detailed issues from the work of a detective, but he also invited me on some of his surveillance missions, and at other times he sent me into the field with his agents. Banal cases of adultery, of course, investigated with a view to divorce proceedings, but this does not matter. Eventually, the following around, the lying in wait, the fixed observation point, the electronic surveillance, the recording, the photographing, the filming, the rummaging in rubbish bags etc. takes place in the same manner, irrespective of the nature of the case. At the end of that he did not want to take any money from me, he said I was going to pay him from the author's rights. As I did not write that novel, not only was he left unpaid, but he was again the one who treated me to a beer in summertime, on a terrace, or a finger-width of whisky during the colder seasons, in the evening at his office situated on the ground floor of a block in the town centre. He also had a bigger head office, somewhere closer to the periphery, where the rest of the offices, equipment storerooms, and places for the training of his detectives etc. were to be found.

In the time it took me to remember all this, Max had already appeared, accompanied by two of his young employees. Perfectly undercover! They had already undressed, probably at the entrance of the lido, so they appeared in bathing trunks, carrying in one hand some bags which contained their clothing, along with a beach towel in the other. All three had very dark sunglasses. I remembered: the colour and shape of the eyes are easiest to recall. When I worked with him, he told me that he also had contact lenses for his agents, but they preferred not to torment their eyes unless it was absolutely necessary. They found me easily, as I realised, coming towards me, stopping at a distance of some fifteen metres on a free patch of sand, spreading their towels one near the other and then stretching out on them in their turn. Max lit a cigarette, the young ones didn't. One of them took out three cans of beer from a brown bag made of fake leather, then they sat on their bums, opened the cans and started to drink and chatter as if they were work colleagues out of the office or, if we take into account that it was not yet lunchtime, runaways from the office. After finishing the beer, Max looked at me as if by chance, stood up and directed himself to the wooden constructions sheltering the shops where you could buy refreshing drinks, coffee and various hot snacks. I stood up, made my way in the opposite direction, towards one of the men's toilets, went in, lingered a little in the hallway by washing my hands in the sink and splashing water over my face, then I went out and, in a somewhat roundabout manner, made my way to the place where Max had gone a little while earlier. He had bought himself a coffee and was sitting at a wooden table behind the building. I bought one too and sat at the same table, on the bench on the other side. We exchanged a greeting and I told him in a few sentences what this was all about, what I wanted from him. He congratulated himself for the fact they had each arrived in their own car and he told me we were talking about three days of total surveillance, one day for the corroboration of the materials and editing the reports.

We were going to see each other on Monday afternoon, at 17:00, in the garden of a new pub, well hidden by trees and plants, that had opened somewhere in the town centre. "You are in the centre, but you have the sensation there is no town around you", added Max. He then asked me to show him the "objects", the double objectives, if we thought we were talking about couples, and he asked me if I needed binoculars. It was then that I noticed he had taken with him a sort of leather money belt when he had left his towel.

I replied that no, that I had just gotten rid of myopia, but I had switched to the use of glasses with the plus sign. So, as a consequence, I showed him the couples by finding them with the naked eye. He noted them down according to marks known only by him, and then told me that this specific piece of fun would cost me a small fortune. "Good", I replied, "it is not a problem".

He left for his detectives, while I, after I finished my coffee, entered the pool in order to do some laps, since my cause was now in good hands. When I returned to my towel, I noticed Max was no longer there, but the two young detectives were getting toasted in the sun, apparently uninterested by anything around them. After some hour and a bit – it was already lunchtime and the sun was burning – the first couple started to gather their things, a thing also done, somewhat casually, by one of the detectives, who then left for the exit before the couple did. I knew this trick as well, remembering it from the shadowing operations in which I had taken part. I did not wait for the second couple to leave accompanied by their guardian angel. I knew the business would work by itself from then on, and nothing more was left for me to do than to wait for the report and Monday afternoon's discussion with Max. Getting dressed, I gathered my things and started lazily for the exit. On my way there, I stopped and bought a cold Pepsi Light, which I started to drink in slow mouthfuls.

On Monday, a little while before 17:00 hours, I found the garden of the new pub, which was located indeed within a kind of Kilometre Zero of the centre, on a little street that started across the road from the lyceum where I had been a pupil. Max was already at a table, in the shade of a kind of arbour which was not very tall, but very rich in branches and leaves, an ornamental arbour whose name totally eluded me. I noticed again that, no matter the hour when I got to a meeting, Max was already there, so much so that I started to believe he had waited for me for hours on end, if not days. He had an alcohol-free beer in front of him and a bowl of roasted and salted peanuts. A lively waitress came by and I ordered a Mexican beer made of maize and rice. Max said that I had good taste. I replied that I suffered from diabetes! From a flat briefcase, but not of the "diplomat" model which is so embarrassing, he took out two thin files of some 15 pages each, with the text edited in 14-size fonts on the computer. He also took out a box in which there had probably been toner cartridges and he said to me: "Photographs, audio tapes. We did not film as it was no need". I wanted to look over what he'd given me, but he told me I should consult them at home, and when I no longer needed them, I should destroy them. He had stepped over many paragraphs from the law regarding the protection of private life. He also said he had edited the reports so that they would look like pages in a work of fiction. We had finished our beers, so we ordered another round, drinking while the discussion had taken a slide towards politics. I took out the wallet and asked him: "How much?". He replied it was sufficient to pay the modest order at the bar, and that, although he knew almost nothing of my literature, he was constantly reading my articles in the papers. He had even noted down some things from them in a thick notebook in which he writes things that attract his attention. He also said that he actually wanted something. When we both had the time, I should explain to him how things are with the birth of modernity, the values around which it functions and why our society is not one which is truly modern. And why do I call it extra-modern, and not pre-modern. He had read an article of mine, but it was short, without details. I told him I would send by email a longer essay from which that actual article had started, and that we should talk about these themes afterwards. The girl came by, I paid and I left on my way, while he stayed there, sitting at the table. He arrives first, he leaves last. Or perhaps he had another appointment arranged for that place. It wouldn't have been one "for work"; he had told me once that you should never have two meetings in the same place without a period of pause between them. On the road, I said to myself: what a damn business, the former *Securitate* has started to support the arts and he is also bettering itself through my coaching!

Once I reached home, I placed the files and the box on the little table in the wicker kiosk behind the house, in the spot which was most protected from the glare of the sun during the course of the greater part of the day. Then I went inside, filled a cup of coffee and poured into a glass two finger widths of Uncle Jack – as I call Mr Daniel out of love and respect. I looked first at the photos, which told me almost nothing, with the exception of three with the *fausse maigre* in the bathing suit – yes, she did look good! – and one in which my Apollo was accompanied by a man around fifty years of age who had placed his hand, somehow protectively, on the shoulder of the younger man, and seemed to be talking to him with a certain passion. In fact, these were three photos, but taken so fast, one after the other, that it required a bit of an effort to see that they were different frames.

I started to read the reports, stopping from time to time in order to insert a tape in my old Philips cassette player, which was bought during one of my first exits abroad, around 1990 or 1991. On a white label, each tape wore the essential information, in numbers: 1 or 2 for the couples, the second number, from 1 to 3, signalling the day of surveillance, and the third being the hour when the recording had been made. Simple and efficient, so you could match without any errors the appropriate tape with passages in the reports. Now, of course, if I wanted to prolong the story for no reason, I could transcribe the surveillance reports in their entirety – even as they were, Max had edited them as if they were parts of a work of fiction. I do not want to prolong the story, nor would I like to appropriate another man's work, especially since it had been left unpaid. I think Max has a liking for me, or, purely and simply, as he said to me once in jest – or that's what I believed! – he is getting ready to appoint me as a partner, but I could prolong the story without stealing another man's goods, introducing, for example, a theorising passage in which I would explain the intermingling of real and grammatical times and tenses in the prose I write. On the other hand, I do not like offering things already prepared to the readers, like putting berries straight in their mouths, and I like even less to make that offer to the literary critics. So, without going on any longer, my initial conclusions were leagues away from what the surveillance operation established. In spite of his placid appearance, George, the man in the first couple, seemed to be incredibly well loved by his beautiful partner. He is not a state or financial clerk, but an IT worker and even a highly performing one. In their intimacy, the *fausse maigre* woman calls him "my teddy bear", and if we check out at his performances, as they come out from the recordings, I think he is rather a giant bear! In the case of the second couple, it is she who flies from flower to flower. In three days, she cheated on Apollo twice; with the same man, it is true, who, aesthetically speaking, could not even reach the ankle of the legitimate partner. Nevertheless, as the recordings show, this latter has some erectile dysfunction and a sort of penchant for men. No, the surveillance had not caught him in any flagrant event, but the meeting with the slightly older man, the occasion on which the photos had been taken, had a certain ambiguity. I looked again at the three successive frames. There is no doubt that you could perceive a certain ambiguity in the postures of the characters. Looking more, I recognised a theatre actor about whom such rumours circulated. I only knew him from the stage, which is why I had such difficulty identifying him. Anyway, this was also written in the report, in a few lines after mentioning the scene and the photographs.

My conclusions were turned on their head. It is true that the new ones, resulting from the investigation, can lead to a more interesting story. The truth is that I do not know what to do with my characters and with the outline of their story. Should I go with my first impressions? They had proven incorrect, and I had proposed to myself to be as honest as I can with my readers. Should I make appeal to the results of the investigation? Should I imagine something else? For example, that the *fausse maigre* and Apollo know each other, that they are even in a relationship and they had arranged to come to the lido at the same time in order to launch signs of love under the eyes of their legitimate partners? The truth is that, when you have something to write, especially a novel that requires a lot of concentration and a lot of work, it is easier to give up, to not write. This is how I acted some years ago on the police-procedural novel which occasioned my first meeting with Max. Or, at least, it's easier to postpone its writing as much as you can. For the moment, I have the impression that my dive into reality is not sufficient, that my documentation is still approximate. I am thinking that, after some two more days of documenting at the lido, I should go to other sectors of reality on Sunday, for example to the places of leisure at Breazu or Repedea, where, once again, you can be party to great chunks of meat. I mean to say possible characters, but who are as real as it gets.

10 August 2011

The End

About the author

LIVIU ANTONESEI (born 1953) is a professor at the Faculty of Psychology and Educational Sciences of the Al. I. Cuza University of Iaşi; he is a member of the Romanian al PEN Club and ASPRO (The Association of Professional Writers); he is the founder of the cultural magazine Timpul (The Time).

His literary debut took place in 1988 with *Semnele timpului* (Signs of the Time). Other works: *Pharmakon* (poetry, 1989), *Căutarea căutării* (The Search of Searches, poetry, 1990), *Vremea în schimbare* (Times in a State of Change; interviews, 1995), *Apariţia Eonei şi celelalte poeme de dragoste culese din Arborele Gnozei* (The Appearance of Eona and the Other Love Poems Picked from the Tree of Gnosis, 1999), *Nautilus. Structuri, momente şi modele în cultura interbelică* (Nautilus. Structures, Moments and Models in Inter-War Culture, 1999; second edition 2007), *Despre dragoste. Anatomia unui sentiment* (About Love. The Anatomy of a Sentiment, 2000; e-edition 2005; second edition 2010), *Check Point Charlie. Şapte povestiri fără a mai socoti şi prefaţa* (Check Point Charlie. Seven Stories, without Counting the Foreword, 2003), *La Morrison Hotel. Povestiri de pînă azi* (At the Morrison Hotel. Stories until Nowadays, 2007).

At Polirom publishing house he also published: *Jurnal din anii ciumei: 1987-1989. Încercări de psihologie spontană* (Journal from the Years of the Plague: 1987-1989. Attempts at Spontaneous Psychology, 1995), *Paideia. Fundamentele culturale ale educaţiei* (Paideia. Cultural Fundaments of

Education, 1996), *O prostie a lui Platon. Intelectualii și politica* (Plato's Foolishness. Intellectuals and Politics, 1997), *Literatura, ce poveste! Un diptic și cîteva linkuri în rețeaua literaturii* (Literature - What a Story! A Diptych and Some Links in the Network of Literature, 2004), *Polis și Paideia. Șapte studii despre educație, cultură și politici educative* (Polis and Paideia. Seven Studies on Education, Culture and Educational Policies, 2005). In 2013, Liviu Antonesei published a new volume of poetry, *Un taur în vitrina de piatră* (A Bull in the Stone Display).

His most recent short-story collection at Polirom in 2011 is *The Innocent and Collateral Victims of a Bloody War with Russia (Victimele inocente și colaterale ale unui sîngeros război cu Rusia*, 2011).

Always a busy promoter of culture and education, Liviu was also active as the editorial director of Adenium publishing house, and the President of the Festival of Books and Authors for Children and Young Adults in Iași.

PROFUSION GOLD SERIES

Report on the State of Loneliness (Raport asupra singurătății)
by Augustin Buzura
ISBN 13: 9780956867643

A deeply reflexive meditation on the history of Doctor Cassian, from the Second World War to contemporary times in Romania, told through the experiences of a panoply of characters and events. In counterpoint, the novel details the reflections of a young woman, Mara, and her relationship with the doctor.

Augustin Buzura (born 22 September 1938, Berința, Maramureș County, Romania) studied General Medicine in Cluj, and specialised in psychiatry.

In 1963 he made his debut in Bucharest with the collection of stories *Capul Bunei Speranțe* (Cape of Good Hope). In 1964 he renounced the medical profession, becoming an editorial secretary for *Tribuna* (Tribune) magazine. In 1967 he published the second volume of stories, *De ce zboară vulturul?* (Why Does the Eagle Fly?), after which he started building a vast oeuvre.

His novels, *Absenții* (The Absentees, 1970), *Fețele tăcerii* (The Faces of Silence, 1974), *Orgolii* (Pride, 1977), *Vocile nopții* (Voices of the Night, 1980), *Refugii* (Refuges, 1984) and *Drumul cenușii* (The Road of Ashes, 1988), confronted communist censorship, bringing the author celebrity, friendship and solidarity from the readers. *Recviem pentru nebuni și bestii* (Requiem for fools and beasts, 1999) is the novel of the period transition in Romanian society, which Augustin Buzura observed with the same unbiased vigilance. His latest novel, *Raport asupra singurătății* (Report on the

179

State of Loneliness, 2009), explores the Romanian landscape over more than seventy years, subtly locating the history of a myriad of individuals and events within their broader European context. All his novels enjoyed countless editions in Romania and abroad, and gained the author numerous prizes.

In addition, Buzura is a practitioner of other literary genres, essays (*Bloc notes* - Notepad, 1981) and memoirs (*Tentația risipirii* - The Temptation of Dissipation, 2003). In 2003 he published *Teroarea iluziei. Convorbiri cu Crisula Ștefanescu* (The Terror of Illusion. Conversations with Crisula Ștefanescu).

He is also a stalwart of Romanian journalism. In addition to *Tribuna*, Augustin Buzura wrote for almost all the Romanian literary magazines, founding several publications under the aegis of the Romanian Cultural Foundation, an organisation he led as president until 2003. His recent volume, *Nici vii, nici morți* (Neither Alive, Nor Dead, 2012) is the best illustration of Buzura's credo, opposing truth to rhetoric, and unmasking the political masquerades of the moment.

President of the Romanian Cultural Institute until January 2005, he re-launched, in the same year, the magazine *Cultura* (Culture), which he leads as editor-in-chief and editorialist. He holds honorary Doctorates from the Lucian Blaga University of Sibiu and the University of Baia Mare. He is also a correspondent member of Sudosteuropa Gesellschaft and a member of the Romanian Academy, the Brazilian Academy of Letters and the Academy of Latinity.

PROFUSION GOLD SERIES

Greuceanu – Novel with a Policeman (Greuceanu - roman [cu un] politist) by Stelian Ţurlea
ISBN 13: 9780956867667

Writer and philosopher Stelian Ţurlea based his crime fiction 'Greuceanu' on a well-known Romanian fairytale, in which the eponymous hero battles with a number of Zmei [ogres], to bring back to the skies the sun which they had stolen. The novel transposes the fairytale to the reality of a provincial town which has been taken over by gangsters, now the town's masters. Greuceanu is a young policeman, at the bottom of the ladder. By chance, he gets rid of one of the feared gangsters, whose brothers and their wives come after him. Greuceanu defeats them all, and, as in the fairytales, he marries the emperor's daughter - in this case, the daughter of the town's mayor. With the unerring instinct of a popular children's author, Ţurlea locates, in Greuceanu, one of the major Pan-European issues in contemporary times, the problem of organised crime. Ţurlea's villains are not moustachioed banditos. Instead they are the brothers and sisters of gangsters in every European city centre, and playing as he does with the characters of the town, he explores a number of insights into the role of organised crime in post-Accession civic life.

"Greuceanu is a paper cop from the archives, but he steps out of them in order to fight those who rule by robbery and criminality. As in the case of the policeman-archivist, appearances are deceptive with Stelian Ţurlea. The dark and massive editorialist is a sprightly prose writer, quick to make jokes, skilful in constructing a plot which he complicates progressively, seemingly in order to have better fun at the final disentanglement of all the knots." (Horia Gârbea – Luceafărul, Săptămâna financiară)

Born in January 1946, Stelian Țurlea studied Philology (1968) and Philosophy (1976) in Bucharest. For nearly three decades, he has been editor on external affairs ("Lumea" magazine). After 1989, he has coordinated "Lumea", "Zig-Zag", and "Meridian" magazines, and worked in television as Head of Antena 1 News Department. He has been working for ProTV since 1996 and, since 2000, he has been a senior editor for "Ziarul de duminică".

He is the author of eighteen novels, ten books on journalism, nine books for children and two translations. He has coordinated six photo albums (a three-volume album about Bucharest during Carol I; other albums: The public works during Carol I; The Palace of the Patriarchy; The Royal Palace; B.N.R. – Chronicle of the Old Palace Restoration; The Financial-Banking, Historical Centre of Bucharest).

He received the Writers' Union Award for Children's Literature (2003), the Romanian Editors' Association Award for Children's Literature (2005), the Writers' Union Special Award (2006) and the Bucharest Writers' Association Award (2007), Flacăra Prize for Literature (2011). He was nominated for the Writers' Union Award for Children Literature in 2000 and the AER Novel Award in 2003.

NOIR FROM EASTERN EUROPE
from Profusion.org.uk

Profusion brings you an extraordinary trio of crime fiction novels from Romanian authors in English translation, plus an amazing true crime book:

Attack in the Library (*Atac în bibliotecă*) by George Arion, one of the classic narratives of Romanian crime fiction, was written during the dictatorship of the 1980s in the finest Noir tradition.
"I loved this book. Dry, snappy, absurdist wit... the colossal, surreal stupidity of totalitarianism."
Patrick McGuinness – author, The Last Hundred Days – Man Booker Prize Longlist

Kill the General (*Ucideți generalul*) by Bogdan Hrib, an exciting and suspenseful thriller, takes you on a rollercoaster ride through the last decades in Romanian history.
"...a good read offering an insight into a country that remains mysterious to many of us."
Julian Cole – The Press, York

Anatomical Clues (*Indicii anatomice*) by Oana Stoica-Mujea features Iolanda, a crime-fighting heroine unique in the landscape of Romanian literature: mad, bad and dangerous to know.
"...a gripping tale, which, like Iolanda, will creep into your head and stay there."
Mike Phillips – author, CWA Silver Dagger winner

Rimaru - Butcher of Bucharest (*Rîmaru – Măcelarul Bucureștiului*) by Mike Phillips and Stejarel Olaru is a social review of Romania in the 70s, with a serial killer's story as a central focus.

"... a fascinating read that frames a factual account of the crimes within their social environment, while examining their impact on the culture, and their lingering legacy in the present day."
George Nott – Enfield INDEPENDENT

All Profusion books are available in paperback from Profusion.org.uk and Amazon.co.uk, as well as Kindle e-books.

PROFUSION CRIME SERIES - Fiction/Non-Fiction, Series Editor: Dr Mike Phillips OBE
Profusion Publishers - An Independent British Publishing House, based in London.